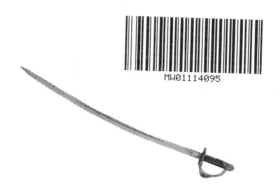

THE BATTLE
OF WATERLOO

J. Christopher Herold

HORIZON • NEW WORD CITY

Published by New Word City, Inc.

For more information about New Word City, visit our Web site at
NewWordCity.com

American Heritage Publishing
Edwin S. Grosvenor, President
P.O. Box 1488
Rockville, MD 20851

1

RISE AND FALL OF AN EMPEROR

One day late in April 1814, a small procession of dusty carriages rattled into the small town of Orgon in southern France and came to a halt at an inn where fresh horses were waiting to replace the tired ones. In front of the inn stood a hurriedly-made gallows, and from it swung a uniformed dummy, daubed with blood, a placard nailed to its chest: "This, sooner or later, will be the tyrant's end." From every side, a furious, cursing mob pushed and shoved around the largest of the carriages. Inside it, a short, rather fat man was cowering in his seat, trying to hide behind one of his travel companions.

A band of frenzied women, their faces distorted with hatred, their hands scrabbling at the doors, screamed that the man in the carriage was a murderer, the butcher of their sons and husbands. Amid shouts of "Death to the tyrant!", shots rang out and riddled the dangling effigy. Sweat began to glisten on the stout man's already-pale face. Another of his companions, a Russian officer, leaped onto the footboard of the carriage and managed to make himself heard above the roar of the crowd. "Leave him to himself," the officer shouted. "Look at him! Can't you see that contempt is the only weapon you ought to use on this man? He is dangerous no longer!"

The words had their effect; the excited crowd broke into cheering. The coachmen hastily harnessed the fresh horses, and the line of carriages clattered off through the narrow streets. Once safely out of town, the small fat man turned to the Russian and thanked him for having saved his life.

The little man who had so nearly been lynched was the greatest conqueror and military hero of modern times. Until only a few days earlier, his proud titles had been Napoleon I, by the grace of God and the will of the people Emperor of the French, King of Italy, and Protector of the Confederation of the Rhine. For fifteen years, Napoleon Bonaparte had ruled France; for fifteen years, he had been the most talked-about and most feared man in Europe.

Hundreds of thousands of men had died in his campaigns or had returned from them crippled and broken. He had wanted to rule the world, and now he was on his way to exile on the tiny Mediterranean island of Elba, between Corsica and the northwest coast of Italy, where he would be master of only eighty-six square miles of rocky earth and 12,000 peasants and fishermen. It seemed as if the vast armies of Frenchmen who had marched with him across Europe had been killed and mutilated in vain.

Napoleon had never shown fear in battle, but it is one thing to face bullets and shells and quite another to face a mob howling for blood. In the first week of his journey to Elba, he had even joked with his companions about his downfall. "After all," he said humorously, "I've lost nothing, for I began the game with a six-franc piece in my pocket, and I've come out of it very rich."

After the incident at Orgon, however, Napoleon joked no more and thought of nothing but his own safety. He amazed his escort of four commissioners from the victorious Allied powers - Britain, Russia, Austria, and Prussia - by taking on all sorts of grotesque disguises to avoid being recognized. All four escorts were generals in their respective armies, and they were shocked at such cowardice in a man they had thought was a hero.

At one point, Napoleon had posed as one of his own outriders; at another, as the British commissioner. Finally, he put on the Austrian's tunic, the Prussian's cap, the Russian's cloak, and took refuge in the corner of the Austrian commissioner's carriage. First he called up to the coachman on the box to light up his pipe and puff away at it as he drove along. Then he commanded the Austrian general to sing in order to reinforce the impression that the carriage carried no one of any importance. The general protested that he could not sing. "Then whistle," ordered Napoleon - and the general did. Not until he boarded the British ship that was to take him to Elba did Napoleon feel safe.

No man had risen higher or fallen lower. His career seemed finished. Yet only ten months after his arrival in Elba, he was to set out again, practically singlehanded, to recover what he had lost. That amazing adventure was to be Napoleon's last great gamble. To understand what was at stake for him and for the European countries that had become his bitter enemies, it is necessary to recall the events leading to the exile at Elba.

Napoleon's career was one of the most extraordinary in history. It was made possible because he lived in extraordinary times. In 1789, when Napoleon Bonaparte was twenty years old, the French people began the great revolution that was to send their king and queen to the guillotine and to threaten every other monarchy in Europe with the rallying cry of "Liberty, Equality, Fraternity." Napoleon was then an obscure lieutenant of artillery, the son of a genteel but poor family from the French island of Corsica.

If the French Revolution had not shaken the structure of France and of Europe to the foundations, Napoleon might have ended his life with no higher rank than that of captain or major. But by 1793, the chief powers of Europe - Britain, Austria, Spain, Holland, and Prussia - were at war with revolutionary France, which barely had a stable government, let alone an army to face the onslaught.

Traditionally, officers in the royalist army were from aristocratic families, but many of them had fled as the revolution grew in intensity. The revolutionary government had begun drafting conscripts by the thousands to form an "army of the people," but it was badly equipped and desperately in need of discipline and leadership. This situation naturally offered a great opportunity to young and ambitious men - officers and soldiers alike - to show their abilities and earn rapid promotion.

Napoleon, who never missed an opportunity, seized this one. By a stroke of luck, he found himself, only a captain, in virtual command of the artillery besieging Toulon, the great naval base in southern France. The city was held by a joint force of royalist sympathizers and British seamen. The young captain's brilliant strategy was largely responsible for the fall of the town and its total evacuation by the British, and he was promoted to brigadier general as a reward. He was only twenty-four years old.

A couple of years later, in 1796, he was given command of an army - a tattered and starving army of 30,000 men. With inspiring words and the promise of plunder from the fertile plains of northern Italy (which was then controlled by Austria), Napoleon whipped them into shape. Victory followed victory. Austria was forced to make peace in 1797 on terms that gave France all of Belgium and the territory bordering the left bank of the Rhine. Spain. Prussia, and Holland had already withdrawn from the war against revolutionary France. Only Britain continued the struggle.

At twenty-eight, General Bonaparte was the hero of Europe, admired even by his former enemies. But his ambition did not rest there. If France could gain a foothold in the eastern Mediterranean, he realized, she could threaten Britain's great possessions in India. The ideal area for France to take over was Egypt, which was a part of the Ottoman Empire, ruled in the name of the Sultan of Turkey by a corrupt military government. The young general accepted the command of a 35,000-man expeditionary force.

In the summer of 1798, he sailed in a colossal convoy to Egypt, successfully dodging the British fleet under Admiral Sir Horatio Nelson that was cruising the Mediterranean to intercept him. In three weeks of brilliant campaigning, Napoleon conquered the whole of Egypt. But ten days after the French army had marched into Cairo, the capital, Nelson annihilated the French fleet at the Battle of the Nile. Cut off from home, the great expedition to the Orient was doomed.

Encouraged by the British naval victory, the European powers formed a fresh alliance against France. War broke out on the Continent once again, and the French - this time without Napoleon - suffered defeat after defeat. It was touch and go whether their tottering government would be overthrown by the Allied powers or by forces within France itself. Some Frenchmen now wanted to restore the monarchy while others planned to seize power for themselves. Food was scarce. The treasury was nearly empty, and ordinary citizens, hungry and discontented, longed for peace and a return to law and order.

Despite the British blockade of Egypt, Napoleon had kept in touch with what was going on. Ruthlessly, he abandoned his army in Egypt and returned immediately to France. In November 1799, one month after his return, he overthrew the government in Paris with a mere handful of soldiers and the help of a few politicians who saw the little Corsican general as an ideal instrument to gain their own ends. But Napoleon had his own plans, and the politicians found themselves assisting in the election of a new government that was a virtual dictatorship. At its head, with the title of First Consul, was Napoleon Bonaparte. He instantly set about using his enormous powers to remedy the problems facing France from outside and from within. In 1801, Napoleon forced Austria to make peace with France. The next year, Britain, too, signed a peace treaty.

Elected for a ten-year period, Napoleon began using his dictatorial powers at home. With an iron hand, he put down the royalist rebels in the western provinces of France. He set up a system of administration that made efficient government possible once more and, with the help of advisers, drew up new codes of civil, commercial, and criminal law that were to become models of legislation throughout the world.

He restored the disrupted finances of the country, and taxes began to be collected once again. One of the uses to which Napoleon put them was the creation of a system of public education. He handed out awards for excellence in order to stimulate activity not only in education but in agriculture and in industrial development Yet he effectively muzzled any opposition to his regime - from royalist sympathizers or from leftist revolutionaries - by strict press censorship and by suppression of any publications that voiced criticism.

The general peace in Europe, however, was really a state of cold war. The island kingdom of Britain was dependent for her great wealth on seafaring trade with her overseas possessions. A belligerent France, with port cities just across the Channel, was a permanent threat not only because of a possible invasion but because of interference with Britain's control of the seas. The British were convinced that Napoleon had agreed to the peace only to gain time for more conquests that would shatter the precarious balance of power in Europe. In 1803, after only a few months of peace, Britain again declared war on France.

A British-backed attempt to murder Napoleon provided him with the opportunity to take one more step toward absolute power. He had already been proclaimed First Consul for life, but he had no heir; he must found a dynasty. By a unanimous vote in the Senate, backed by a national plebiscite, Napoleon was proclaimed Emperor of the French, and the imperial title was made hereditary in his family. On December 2, 1804, the coronation ceremony was held in the cathedral of Notre Dame in Paris.

His new title did not prevent the established rulers of Europe from continuing to regard Napoleon as a usurper, and a dangerous one. At the same time, it made the former French revolutionists and republicans think of him as a tyrant and a traitor to their cause. Only by waging more wars and winning more victories could he frighten the timid, keep the greedy on his side, and dazzle the French people with the glory and power he could offer their beloved country.

Even before the Egyptian expedition, the French had begun planning an invasion of Britain, and for at least two years, Napoleon had been building vast quantities of flat-bottomed transports and concentrating thousands of his best troops in the Channel ports. But Britain had a large enough fleet to carry on a reasonably effective blockade of every significant French port. Early in 1805, the Toulon squadron of the French fleet under Admiral Pierre Villeneuve succeeded in evading the blockade and joining the fleet of Spain, France's chief ally. Together they led Lord Nelson and his ships on a wild-goose chase across the Atlantic to the Caribbean and then back to the Bay of Biscay. But instead of joining the western French squadron at Brest and attempting to cover the projected invasion of Britain, Villeneuve and his Spanish allies retreated to Cadiz in southwest Spain. There, Nelson's ships at last caught up with them, and on October 21, 1805, destroyed the greater part of the Franco-Spanish fleet at the Battle of Trafalgar. Britain's control of the ocean was complete.

But the emperor had already begun operations on another front. Britain had offered Austria and Russia huge subsidies in return for forming another anti-French coalition on the Continent. Napoleon gave them no time to attack him. His Grand Army was poised at the Channel. He turned it around and, like lightning, marched into Germany where he hurled back the Austrian army, caught completely unawares, at Ulm on October 17. Within six weeks, he had marched into Vienna and crushed the Austro-Russian army at Austerlitz, seventy miles north of the Austrian capital. It was his most brilliant victory, and, most fittingly, it fell on the first anniversary of his coronation.

Austria, which until then had been the most prominent power in Europe, had to make peace at a heavy price. Her ruler, Emperor Francis I, was also Holy Roman Emperor, a title that had originally been conferred by the Pope Leo III upon Charlemagne in the year 800. Although the Holy Roman Empire had once knit together most of central Europe, it had ceased to be a meaningful bond. Napoleon considered himself the true successor to Charlemagne, and he planned to unite Europe in his own fashion. The Holy Roman Empire was dissolved; Francis was forced to abdicate its crown and become simply Emperor of Austria. Napoleon had already made the various states of northern Italy into a united kingdom with himself as king. Now he was able to dethrone the Bourbon King of Naples, whose lands included most of southern Italy as well as Sicily, and give that kingdom to his brother Joseph.

He totally remade the map of Germany, creating a loosely-allied group of states under French "protection" that he called the Confederation of the Rhine. This was eventually to include all the smaller states except Prussia, which occupied most of northern Germany. He crowned kings with abandon, raising his allies, the rulers of Bavaria and Württemberg, to royal rank and making his brother Louis King of Holland.

Meanwhile, King Frederick William III of Prussia, who for years had sat on the fence of neutrality, decided to step down at last. He made an alliance against Napoleon with the Czar of Russia, Alexander I, and persuaded the Elector of Saxony, the state immediately southeast of Prussia, to join him. The Prussian king, a weak monarch at best, had made a fatal error in timing. As the joint Prussian-Saxon forces mobilized to march against Napoleon and his Grand Army, French troops were already in Bavaria ready to strike. On October 14, 1806, in the twin battles of Jena and Auerstedt, Napoleon and his marshal, Louis-Nicolas Davout, wiped out most of the Prussian army. The remainder fled in terror. The king took refuge in his eastern provinces, and Napoleon marched into Berlin, master of yet another kingdom.

After a grueling and costly winter campaign in East Prussia and in Poland against the Russians and the remnants of the Prussian army, Napoleon caught the Russian forces in a bottleneck at Friedland and won a decisive victory on June 14, 1807. Twenty-five thousand Russians were killed or taken prisoner, and Czar Alexander at once sued for peace. At Tilsit, on the Russian frontier, the two emperors met on a raft moored in the middle of the Niemen River and held long secret talks while the King of Prussia, who was not invited to join them, waited on the riverbank in the rain.

The czar was young and idealistic, as full of grandiose plans as Napoleon, although far less able to make them a reality. From an enemy, he suddenly became an admirer and ally of the French emperor. In a secret treaty, they agreed to join forces and divide the world between themselves. They dealt first with Prussia, and the unlucky King Frederick William saw his country become a satellite of France. Moreover, Prussia was forced to cede the part of Poland she controlled; it became the Grand Duchy of Warsaw under the nominal rule of Frederick William's former ally, the Elector - now King - of Saxony. Since Napoleon had forced Saxony to join the Confederation of the Rhine, this really meant that the Grand Duchy of Warsaw was also under the French emperor's control.

Napoleon's goal at last became clearer. He would create an empire that stretched from the Strait of Gibraltar to the Russian border, and France and Russia would divide the Ottoman Empire between them. Paris would become the capital of Europe. Again, Britain stood in the way. Since a direct attack was no longer possible, Napoleon instituted an economic blockade to starve the island into surrendering. He had already issued a decree when he first took Berlin that forbade all trade with the British Isles. For his so-called Continental System to become completely effective, however, he must have control of all the coasts of Europe.

To gain a firmer grip over his principal ally, Spain, he treacherously lured the Spanish royal family into French territory then placed them under arrest and had his brother Joseph proclaimed King of Spain. The husband of Napoleon's sister Caroline, Marshal Joachim Murat, was moved up from a German grand dukedom to replace Joseph as King of Naples. Now the Bonaparte family and their in-laws ruled the larger part of Europe, and the trade war with Britain seemed sure of success.

In the Iberian Peninsula, however, Napoleon had miscalculated. Portugal refused to cut off her profitable British trade, and the Spanish people refused to recognize Joseph as king. Napoleon had dispatched 100,000 men onto the Peninsula, but throughout the barren, rocky country, the population rose in a spontaneous rebellion against the French invaders. Fierce and bloody fighting won the French nominal control over Spain, but bitter guerrilla warfare never ceased. In 1808, Britain sent an expeditionary force to help Portugal. The Peninsular War diverted troops that Napoleon could ill spare from the standing army of nearly 1 million he needed to enforce his domination of Europe. Moreover, it gave an example of patriotic resistance that inspired the other subject nations with fresh hope.

Napoleon consistently underestimated the importance of this struggle in comparison with his other adventures. In 1811, Lord Wellington (Arthur Wellesley), with an army of Englishmen, Portuguese, and Spaniards, began the great offensive that eventually drove the French completely out of Spain. Napoleon himself visited Spain only briefly. He tried to run the war from the other side of Europe by bombarding his brother and his generals with instructions that were weeks out of date by the time they arrived.

As his successes multiplied, the emperor became more and more stubborn, less and less willing to take advice. His alliance with Alexander of Russia cooled quickly. The two emperors fell to quarreling about the division of spoils from lands they had yet to conquer. The scheme for a joint invasion of Turkey and India was postponed indefinitely.

In 1809, Austria, encouraged by the example of the Spanish patriots, prepared another attempt to shake off the Napoleonic yoke. Napoleon was in Spain, reinforcing Joseph's hold on the throne, but he hastened back across the Pyrenees. Once again he crossed Germany with his Grand Army; for a second time, he occupied Vienna, and again Napoleon routed the Austrians in a murderous battle: Wagram.

In 1810, Napoleon, seemingly at the height of his power, was nevertheless in trouble. The French emperor would never feel secure on his throne as long as Britain still resisted. Pope Pius VII, whose territories Napoleon had just seized and annexed to France, had excommunicated him. Napoleon's own brother Louis, King of Holland, had abdicated his throne rather than subject himself to Napoleon's will. And it was clear by then that if Napoleon lost a single important battle, not only Europe would turn against him but even some members of his own government in France. Above all, his wife, the Empress Josephine, had given him no heir; if he died or was killed, who would succeed him?

This gnawing sense of insecurity forced Napoleon to raise himself even higher and to overreach himself. He ordered Pope Pius VII to be arrested and confined at Savona on the Italian Riviera. Hoping to obtain an heir and to be accepted into the brotherhood of European monarchs, he divorced Josephine and married Archduchess Marie Louise, the daughter of Francis I of Austria. He kept trying to plug holes in his blockade against Britain by bullying his allies and the neutral states into enforcing the boycott of British trade ever more strongly. He ignored their pleas that the Continental System took a heavier toll from them than it did from Britain. With Louis Bonaparte's departure from Holland, Napoleon had already annexed that country to France; now he annexed northwestern Germany as far as Lübeck on the Baltic Sea.

On March 20, 1811, a 101-gun salute boomed out over the streets of Paris, and rejoicing citizens filled the squares and drank the wine that flowed - free - from the fountains. Marie Louise had given birth to a son, to whom Napoleon gave the title of King of Rome. At last, he had established a dynasty, mingling the blood of the ancient house of Hapsburg with that of the Bonaparte upstarts.

Was power his only aim? It probably was not although no man ever held more power. Napoleon wanted not only to make France the greatest nation in the world but to create a united Europe. He had grandiose and noble schemes for organizing a new world system with equal laws and equal opportunities for all, with great overseas colonies that would contribute to Europe's prosperity. He planned vast networks of modern roads and canals, new industries, and new educational systems. Conscious of the greatness of his aims, he became more and more tyrannical in their pursuit. He stubbornly ignored any counsel of moderation, demanded sacrifices of people, and provoked resistance in every country of Europe, including his own. He treated even his most faithful allies brutally. Was he aware of the hatred building up around him? He probably was, but he did not mind being hated so long as he was feared.

Those who were close to Napoleon noticed a general decline of his faculties. He was only forty-one when his son, the King of Rome, was born. Yet his once-lean figure was pudgy, his once-sharp features were bloated, and he seemed incapable of summoning the mental energy and concentration to which he owed his greatness. Once he had won his victories through his genius in using small forces to the best advantage; now he won them by massive assaults and sheer slugging power. Such tactics demanded a great deal of cannon fodder, and 43,000 men had been lost in the Austrian campaign of 1809. As a strategist, Napoleon remained unrivaled, but as a tactician, he was becoming careless.

In 1812, Napoleon made the fateful decision to attack Russia. He hoped by defeating Alexander in one or two decisive battles to win him back as an ally and at long last realize his dream of attacking

India. On June 23, 600,000 Frenchmen, Germans, Austrians, Italians, and Poles, the largest army the world had yet seen, under the command of the French emperor, crossed the Russian border.

The Russians fell back before the invaders, setting fire to their farms and cities as they went until Napoleon's Grand Army, accustomed to living off the land it conquered, was almost starving. At Borodino, the Russians made a heroic stand, and although the result was a victory for Napoleon, the butchery was on an unprecedented scale - the French lost 30,000 men, the Russians well over 45,000. But Borodino changed nothing. The Russians continued to retreat and the French to advance, but their forces were dangerously depleted by thousands of battle casualties, stragglers, and deserters.

On September 14, Napoleon, with an army of fewer than 100,000 effectives, entered Moscow, which had been virtually abandoned by its population. The French marched in an ominous silence through the deserted streets, and in the Kremlin where Napoleon and his staff installed themselves, the ticking of innumerable clocks was the only sound in the empty halls. That night, mysteriously, fires broke out all over Moscow. For four days and three nights, the capital of Russia became a landscape in hell as one wooden building after another roared into flames. Then the looting began, and the few goods saved from the fire were lost.

Although Moscow was now almost useless to him, the Kremlin had escaped the fire, and Napoleon remained there for five more weeks gathering reinforcements. He hoped Alexander would offer to negotiate peace. "The climate is as mild as September at Fontainebleau," he insisted to one veteran of Russian winters who implored him to get his army on the march once more. But no word came from the czar, and on October 18, Napoleon gave the order to retreat.

Weighed down by plunder, shivering in their summer uniforms, and with their boots in shreds, more than 100,000 men and a disorderly mob of thousands of camp followers and refugees began the long journey back. In a nightmare of bitter cold, hunger, and harassment by pursuing Russian Cossacks, barely 50,000 survived. In the panic-stricken crossing of the Berezina River, 25,000 men were lost. As the troops plodded on, the corpses of men and horses, and wagons bearing baggage and booty - the wreckage of an army in despair - littered the snowy ground from Smolensk to the Prussian frontier. The Grand Army had melted away.

Curiously, the defeat seemed to revive Napoleon's energy. On December 5, he abandoned the starving remnants of his army near Vilna in Russia and made the long journey back to Paris in a lightning two-week dash by carriage and by sleigh. Within four months, he had raised another army, 200,000 strong.

Now that it had been proven that he was not invincible, Napoleon's unwilling allies began to drop away - first Prussia where brutal treatment by the French had kindled a spirit of nationalism, then Sweden, ruled by one of Napoleon's marshals, Jean Bernadotte, who lost no time in turning against his former commander. As the months went by, Bavaria, Württemberg, Saxony, and in the end, even Naples, under his brother-in-law Murat, were all to desert him.

But Europe still had good reason to fear Napoleon. He began his 1813 campaign with a swift march into Saxony and Silesia, inflicted several important defeats on the Allies, and recaptured Dresden. But his enemies were close to their reinforcements while his army - with no hope of reinforcement - was dwindling. Through his foreign minister, Prince Klemens von Metternich, Francis of Austria made an attempt at mediation with his son-in-law, but it collapsed, and Austria joined the Allies. In a three-day battle that began on October 16, the French army was beaten at Leipzig by the combined armies of Russia, Austria, Prussia, and Sweden - not counting the Saxons who went over to the Allies in mid-battle. Even so, with his 190,000 men, Napoleon managed to inflict such heavy losses on the 300,000-man Allied army that it could not pursue him effectively. With barely half his troops left, he retreated across the Rhine into France. The generals in charge of the campaign, notably Marshal Gebhard Leberecht von Blücher and General August Neithardt von Gneisenau of Prussia, wanted to pursue him, but the sovereigns hesitated and offered peace terms. Napoleon ignored their offer, and on December 22, the Allies reluctantly began sending troops across the Rhine.

Meanwhile, Napoleon had raised yet another army. He had already had to anticipate the draft of 1814 to get enough troops to fight his 1813 battles; now he called upon the boys due for service in 1815. The popular name for these young, beardless lads was "Marie Louises," but they fought most bravely. Napoleon, now down to his last reserves, abandoned the slugging methods of the past years and reverted to the brilliant tactics of his earliest campaigns. For three months, he held at bay the joint Russian, Prussian, and Austrian armies converging on Paris from the north and east. Yet it was a fight against all hope. Wellington, whose series of successes against the French in the Peninsula had brought him every honor his grateful country could heap upon him including a dukedom, was advancing across the Pyrenees into southern France.

On March 9, 1814, Blücher and the Prussian army won a decisive victory over the French at Laon, seventy-five miles northeast of Paris, and began to march directly on the capital. On March 12, Wellington entered Bordeaux, the chief city of southwest France. By March 30, the Allied armies were on the outskirts of Paris. The next day, the city capitulated, and Napoleon fled to Fontainebleau where his marshals finally forced him on April 4, to offer to abdicate in favor of his infant son.

But the Allies were uncertain whom to place upon his vacant throne. Should they appoint Marie Louise regent for her son or should they perhaps elect one of Napoleon's marshals to replace him? Emperor Francis was not averse to seeing his grandson become ruler of France, but the British favored the restoration of the Bourbon monarch Louis XVIII, brother of the guillotined Louis XVI, who had been living quietly in Britain as king in name only. Czar Alexander preferred Louis's cousin, the Duke of Orleans. In their indecision, an interesting personality saw his chance.

Charles Maurice de Talleyrand-Périgord had resigned as Napoleon's foreign minister in 1807. Able, ambitious, and totally unscrupulous, he had even then foreseen the ruin of his master's hopes and had devoted himself to paving the way for the restoration of the Bourbon monarchy with himself as chief minister. He succeeded in persuading Czar Alexander that Louis XVIII's claim to the throne must be honored, and with the czar's consent,

Talleyrand formed a provisional government whose first act was to formally depose Napoleon. The emperor's hopes of founding a dynasty and passing on his imperial title to the three-year-old King of Rome, proved futile, and he abdicated unconditionally on April 6. Marie Louise and the child were soon afterward taken into Austrian custody, and he was never to see either of them again.

On April 11, by the Treaty of Fontainebleau, Napoleon gave up the throne both in his name and in that of his family. As compensation, he received the island of Elba, not far from his native Corsica, as a sovereign principality and the promise of an annual payment, from France, of 2 million francs. Somewhat satirically, he was also allowed to retain the title of emperor - of Elba. On April 20, in the courtyard of the palace of Fontainebleau, he took leave of his beloved Old Guard. He said a few simple words and embraced, first, the Guard's commander and then the colors they had borne to victory in so many battles. As he turned to enter the carriage that would take him to exile, the veterans of his campaigns sobbed unashamedly.

2

THE EXILE RETURNS

In Elba, the man who had ruled Europe busied himself as best he could with administering the tiny principality that was his prison. With no sense of its being a little ridiculous, he held court with the same ceremony as he had in Paris and supervised every last detail of the island's finances, its public buildings and roads, the proper working of its iron mines, and the improvement of its little capital, Portoferraio. He drilled the miniature army of some 600 imperial guardsmen and a couple of squadrons of Polish lancers, which he had been allowed to take with him, and designed a flag for the Elban navy (ten small boats and 129 sailors). Members of his family came to visit him; so did inquisitive tourists and others, described by the resident British commissioner as "mysterious adventurers and disaffected characters from France and Italy." Elba's emperor conversed with them all at great length.

These occupations were not enough to fill the life of a man of Napoleon's gifts - for even a middle-aged and tired Napoleon had more energy than most other men at the peak of their strength. As long as there was a reasonable hope of returning to power, he would not resign himself to living out his life in Elba. When he went into exile, his supporters had adopted the violet - which blooms in the spring - as an emblem of his speedy return. The news that he received from the Continent, and particularly from France, encouraged him in his hopes. From the visitors who came to see him as a curiosity, from the secret emissaries, and from the stream of letters and reports, he drew the same conclusions. Public opinion had changed in France; a large part of the population would welcome him back, and the victorious Allied powers were too divided to oppose him.

At least as far as France was concerned, there was a great deal of truth in these reports. The French nation, to be sure, was tired of war; however, much glory went with it. Yet people had begun to appreciate the political rights they had gained over the past twenty-five years and the equality of opportunity Napoleon had offered them. A new property-owning class had been created by the revolution. Many Frenchmen had bought up, at advantageous prices, the lands and buildings that had been confiscated from the Church and from the nobles who had emigrated abroad, and they were determined not to return them.

Louis XVIII, who returned to Paris on May 3, 1814, was quite aware of the state of public opinion. Although his supporters wished it, the king knew that the revolution simply could not be undone. Even before his return, he had acknowledged this by promising to rule as a constitutional monarch, with his limited powers subject to the will of the people. The citizens of Paris received him cordially, and his reign had a promising beginning.

Although he had spent half his life in exile - in Germany, in Poland, in Lithuania, in England - Louis had acquired wisdom and tolerance from his misfortune. An aging, immensely fat man, almost paralyzed by gout, he had no wish for revenge and hoped only to reign in peace. He granted the people of France a constitutional charter that gave them far more political freedom than they had had under Napoleon's regime. He not only kept the laws that the preceding governments had introduced but also retained most of the Napoleonic generals and administrators. He even refrained from prosecuting those who in 1793 had voted for the execution of his brother, Louis XVI.

But he was surrounded by men less tolerant than

he, who were, as the saying went, "more royalist than the king." Talleyrand, who had become Louis's foreign minister, once remarked, "They have learned nothing and forgotten nothing." At their head was the king's younger brother and heir, the Comte d'Artois.

In the program of the Ultras, as they came to be known, the king would be restored to absolute power. All the confiscated properties of the Church and the *émigré* nobles would have to be returned to them by their purchasers; the existing military and civilian officials would be replaced by *émigrés*; and the feudal privileges of the nobles would be restored to them at least in part. Everything that had happened since 1789 was to be wiped out.

Louis XVIII wisely resisted the Ultras' pressure in most matters, but he had to make some concessions to those who had remained loyal to him during a quarter-century of exile. The flag of the revolution - the blue, white, and red tricolor - was replaced by the traditional standard of the Bourbons: gold fleurs-de-lis on a white ground. This was an insult to all the men of the victorious armies that had carried the revolutionary banner to Brussels, Milan, Rome, Cairo, Vienna, Berlin, Warsaw, Madrid, and Moscow.

The larger part of the army was demobilized, the veteran officers were retired at half pay, and the Imperial Guard was replaced by the king's household troops whose noble officers had never fought in battle. Such measures naturally aroused discontent among the out-of-work officers who were the chief sufferers. The nation as a whole, moreover, feared that these moves might be evidence of the new regime's reactionary tendencies and that their precious personal liberty was in danger.

To many Frenchmen, Napoleon was no longer the tyrant and butcher he had seemed only a few months earlier. He was the son of the revolution and the champion of common-sense liberalism against feudal ideas of a bygone age. He had created the Code Napoleon, the civil code of laws that had spread the principle of equality beyond the Rhine and the Alps into Germany and Italy. His most popular slogan had been *la carrière ouverte aux talents* - "careers open to all talents" - and in his government, men of the lowliest birth had risen to the highest posts. His wars might have been bloody, but they had been fought against the forces of reaction. He was the hero who had given every Frenchman a chance to be a hero. It was Napoleon's awareness of this shift of public opinion in his favor - or, at least, against the existing Bourbon regime - that made him risk a return to France.

In addition, the general European situation was still quite unsettled. Napoleon had toppled monarchies, altered frontiers, and introduced new laws and systems of administration until hardly a country in Europe was left the way he had found it. Talleyrand had suggested the principle on which the victorious Allies decided to restore order - the principle of legitimacy. This meant that they committed themselves to re-establishing, as far as possible, the state of things that had existed before the abolition of the French monarchy in 1792. But, of course, this was more easily said than done.

Reaching an Allied peace settlement with France, however, was easier than might have been expected. Since the Allies would only be making it difficult for their protégé, Louis XVIII, if they treated France as a defeated enemy, they decided to be generous. No war indemnities were imposed, and Allied troops were to be withdrawn completely. Even the countless art treasures that Napoleon had looted from every country in Europe were to remain in France for the time being, for fear of wounding French pride. As for a decision on a general European settlement, that was left to a congress of nations to be held in Vienna in the autumn of 1814.

The treaty that had finally brought peace to France had been signed by Spain, Portugal, and Sweden in addition to the four principal powers: Britain, Austria, Prussia, and Russia. Naturally, the three smaller nations expected a voice in the deliberations to be held in Vienna. But the Big Four had agreed in a secret treaty to make all the important decisions themselves - and had no intention of sharing their control of Europe's destiny with Spain, Portugal, or Sweden, let alone with the multitude of rulers, delegations from smaller countries, and representatives of different religious and economic interests who soon began flocking into Vienna. On the other hand, the basis for the great powers' domination of the Congress was very flimsy since they were not given executive responsibility by any formal treaty but had usurped it by a secret alliance.

Talleyrand, who was in Vienna to represent Louis XVIII and the interests of France, was quick to bring his crafty and logical arguments to bear on the illegality of the Allies' position, and he successfully won France a place in their council. Once the Council of Four became a Council of Five, Talleyrand's objections to its making all the decisions at the Congress speedily vanished.

Much was expected from the Congress of Vienna - perhaps too much. Each of the principal nations had its own ideas about what should happen to the frontiers of Europe. When the unifying force of their opposition to Napoleon was gone, it became apparent that the Allies were seriously divided. The difficulty of coming to any agreements put off the formal activity of the Congress for month after month, while committees appointed to handle less controversial matters worked industriously behind the scenes.

Meanwhile, the entertainment of the quantities of distinguished visitors taxed Austrian ingenuity - and finances - to the limit. Emperor Francis I sat down to dinner in the Hofburg palace every night with an emperor, an empress, four kings, one queen, three grand duchesses, and several princes and princesses while the grooms in his stables tended the 1,400 horses that carried the bevy of royalty from one amusement to another. There were feasts, balls, concerts, operas, and brilliant gatherings by the score. In November, Beethoven, old and completely deaf, conducted a gala concert of his works attended by the czar and King Frederick William of Prussia. The coming of snow brought sleighing expeditions by torchlight to the Vienna woods. There was even a balloon ascension, with the flags of all the nations dangling from the balloonist's basket. Lord Castlereagh (Robert Stewart), the British foreign secretary, and his wife conscientiously took dancing lessons. Talleyrand, unable to dance because of his lame leg, held daily receptions while barbers were dressing his hair in the elaborate, powdered style of the previous century. Prince Metternich, the Austrian foreign minister, and Czar Alexander, two exceptionally handsome men, indulged in constant flirtations, some of which brought about rivalries that embittered their relationship at the council table.

Through the glittering scene moved the secret agents of the various powers. They employed housemaids to check the contents of wastebaskets in the apartments of the leading delegates, bribed the diplomatic couriers for the ciphers that were the key to the messages they carried for their governments at home, and wrote minutely-detailed reports to their superiors. From these reports, for example, the Emperor Francis could learn that the czar washed his face and hands each morning with a huge block of ice and that the British mission, "through excessive caution," had, on its own, engaged two housemaids to empty its wastebaskets.

The Congress almost broke up, however, in January 1815, when war seemed imminent over the question of Poland. That unfortunate land had been partitioned into nonexistence in the eighteenth century when Prussia, Austria, and Russia had divided her provinces among them. Prussia's share had been made the Grand Duchy of Warsaw by Napoleon, and the czar now proposed to annex the duchy, supposedly in order to restore Poland to liberty once more. He had secured the support of the King of Prussia by promising him Saxony in return for giving up his Polish provinces.

But Metternich, Castlereagh, and Talleyrand all were fearful of allowing either Russia or Prussia to extend her frontiers too far and threaten the European balance of power as Napoleon had.

Austria, Britain, and France thereupon signed a defensive treaty of alliance against Russia and Prussia. Although it was supposed to be a secret agreement, the czar learned of it and arranged a compromise (mainly at the expense of the unlucky Poles). By March, the Congress had made substantial progress toward re-establishing European stability.

That stability was to last for half a century although the sovereigns and ministers who arranged it paid little regard to the growing sense of national identities within the European continent. Many of their more liberal subjects had hoped for guarantees of constitutional government, political rights, and freedom of the press and of religion. It was not to restore the old order exactly as before that the patriots in Germany had taken up arms against Napoleon. However, instead of the national unity they had hoped for, they were now offered a loose confederation dominated by a greedy Prussia and a reactionary Austria. The small states of Italy had likewise hoped for independence; instead they were once more to be under the thumb of Austria. The Belgians found themselves in an unnatural alliance with their Dutch neighbors to the north as subjects of the King of Holland; the larger country, Britain hoped, would help block any future French invasion attempts across the Channel. Poland was again partitioned among Russia, Prussia, and Austria. Although the Russian portion was to be named a separate kingdom, the Poles would be no more independent than they had been under Napoleon's domination in the Grand Duchy of Warsaw.

In Spain, King Ferdinand VII, after six years' imprisonment in France, was welcomed back by his countrymen in the spring of 1814. He began his reign by abolishing the constitution and persecuting his liberal supporters. During the long war against Napoleon, the Whigs in Britain's Parliament had often sounded more like allies of Bonaparte than members of His Majesty's Loyal Opposition. Liberal opinion there was violently critical of the Tory regime that was fashioning the peace at Vienna.

It seemed almost as if Europe had exchanged the one tyrannical genius of Napoleon for dozens of petty and narrow-minded tyrants.

It was thus logical for Napoleon to think that if he returned to France, the army and part of the nation would welcome him and that the rest would not oppose him. As for the European powers, he believed that their several interests were still in such conflict that they would not unite against him if he could reassure them of his peaceful intentions. In this he underestimated the influence that hereditary rulers still had over the majority of their people, and he overestimated the liberal opinion that, vociferous though it was, formed only a small minority, in all lands.

Nevertheless, two personal considerations helped Napoleon decide to break his agreement with Louis XVIII and return to France. The statesmen in Vienna - Talleyrand among them - were uneasy about Elba's nearness to the mainland. The possibility of sending Napoleon to a safer place, such as the remote island of St. Helena in the southern Atlantic, was being seriously discussed. The emperor considered that this change of plan gave him a valid excuse for breaking his agreement with the Allies. Indeed, in his view, that agreement had already been broken by the French government's refusal to pay him his stipulated annual pension of 2 million francs.

On February 26, 1815, in the utmost secrecy, Napoleon embarked with his Guard and a battalion of Corsican sympathizers - an army barely 1,000 strong - to reconquer France. By an incredible piece of luck, his little seven-boat flotilla escaped detection by the British ships that were cruising off Elba to prevent the emperor's escape. In the afternoon of March 1, Napoleon and his troops landed on a deserted stretch of beach between Fréjus and Antibes. The emperor was on French soil once again.

Never had there been a more daring gamble. Yet the man who chanced it was neither a madman nor reckless in the ordinary sense. Human lives meant nothing to Napoleon if he had to sacrifice them to gain his ends, but he never did anything rash. He calculated everything. This time, the odds were probably against him, and he knew it. Still, there was a good chance of success, and he was a man whose daring, intelligence, energy, and speed enabled him to exploit even the smallest opportunity while his opponents were likely to waste their much bigger ones. This he also knew.

After landing, the miniature invasion force bivouacked on the beach. Before daybreak, under a bright moon, Napoleon and his troops began the march north to Grenoble, keeping to a less-traveled road through the mountains. All the royalist officials of France could do was to relay a message to Paris by semaphore telegraph: "Napoleon has invaded France."

What followed was one of the strangest adventures in history. At Laffrey, the soldiers of the Grenoble garrison barred the road with muskets at the ready. Napoleon stepped forward. "If there is one among you who wishes to kill his emperor, I am here!" he cried, throwing open his gray greatcoat, and the soldiers tumbled over one another in their eagerness to throw down their arms and fall at his feet. Cheering, they accompanied the little army on its way northward.

The mood of the population had changed since those April days of 1814 when Napoleon had almost been lynched. Some - especially the lower classes - received him with enthusiasm; most were indifferent. But the French soldiers were ready to follow him once more, and everywhere along the way, government troops swelled the ranks of the invaders.

After Napoleon passed Grenoble, his march became a triumphant progress. He issued a proclamation to the army: "Come and range yourselves under the flags of your leader! He has no existence except in your existence . . . his interests, his honor, his glory, are none other than your interests, your honor, your glory. Victory will march at a quickstep. The eagle and tricolor shall fly from steeple to steeple to the towers of Notre Dame!"

And, indeed, they did fly from steeple to steeple as the church bells rang out the news of the emperor's return. At Auxerre, however, Napoleon's progress was almost stopped. There, his old comrade Marshal Ney, with 6,000 of the king's troops, was awaiting him. Michel Ney - "the bravest of the brave," as Napoleon had called him - had promised Louis XVIII to bring Bonaparte to Paris in an iron cage, and he had meant it. Yet, as he faced the man whom he had served in so many campaigns, the old emotions overcame him; he fell into Napoleon's arms and brought his troops over to him.

Until Ney's treason - if it may be called that - the government of Louis XVIII had not been overly alarmed by Napoleon's approach. Now it fell into complete panic. All thought of resistance was abandoned. The ministers and the courtiers jumped into their carriages and drove off, forgetting even to take the state papers with them or to burn them. During the night of March 19, the king himself slipped out of the Tuileries palace like a thief and began a flight that took him and his court all the way to Ghent in Belgium. The following day, Napoleon entered Paris in triumph. The tricolor was flying from the towers of Notre Dame, and the cathedral's huge bells were ringing. He had won the first round of his gamble, and what was later to be called the Hundred Days had begun.

3
THE HUNDRED DAYS
BEGIN

At 6:00 a.m. on March 7, 1815, Prince Metternich, who had gone to bed only two hours earlier after an unusually late session of the Congress of Vienna, was roused by a valet with a sealed message. The exhausted diplomat took the envelope - bearing an express dispatch from the Austrian consul in Genoa - and laid it on his bedside table for consideration in the morning. But Metternich found he could not get to sleep again. Finally, at about 7:30, he opened the envelope. It contained a six-line message: the British commissioner from Elba had entered Genoa harbor inquiring whether anyone had seen Napoleon, who had disappeared from his island prison. Upon being told "No," the commissioner had immediately put to sea.

Throwing on his clothes, Metternich hastened to show the dispatch to the Austrian emperor. He had long feared that Napoleon would escape from an island so perilously close to Europe. But Francis read the message unhurriedly. "Napoleon appears anxious to run great risks," Metternich later quoted the emperor as saying. "That is his business. Ours is to give to the world that repose which he has troubled all these years. Go at once and find the Emperor of Russia and the King of Prussia; tell them that I am prepared to order my armies once again to take the road to France. I have no doubt that the two sovereigns will join me in my march."

At 8:15, Metternich received the czar's assent to the plan; by 8:30, he had an assurance from King Frederick William of Prussia as well. By 9:00 a.m., he was back in his own house and had already sent for Prince Karl Philipp von Schwarzenberg, field marshal of the Austrian army. As the strokes of ten sounded from the clock towers of Vienna, aides-de-camp were galloping out of the city with instructions for their various army corps, and the ministers of the Council of Five began to assemble in Metternich's study. "In this way," the prince ended his account of that eventful morning, "war was decided on in less than an hour."

The news of Napoleon's landing in France fell like a bombshell upon the lesser delegates and hangers-on at the Congress. "A thousand candles seemed in a single instant to have been extinguished," wrote one observer. "The Congress is dissolved," Napoleon himself had proclaimed as he stepped ashore. His boast, however, was premature.

The emperor had calculated - quite correctly - that the Bourbon regime in France would collapse almost at the sound of his name. He also expected to take advantage of the dissension among the Allied powers that had brought them to the brink of war as recently as January. In France, he would pose as the champion of the people against the reactionary monarch, Louis XVIII. Elsewhere in Europe, he would appear to be a peace-loving man with no intention of renewing the war - the only ruler firm enough to prevent a second French revolution.

Napoleon's eager calculations, however, overlooked the considerable strides toward a settlement that had been taken at Vienna since the January quarrel had been smoothed over. He also ignored the possibility that his arrival in France, far from increasing the rift between the Allies, might stir them to sudden unity in the face of a common threat. Of course, that is exactly what happened. Napoleon's probably sincere hope that he could avoid, or at least postpone, war was immediately destroyed.

On March 13, Austria, France, Great Britain, Prussia, Russia, Spain, Portugal, and Sweden jointly issued a call to arms against Napoleon whom they declared an outlaw and a "disturber of world repose." The Duke of Wellington, who had only recently succeeded Castlereagh as Britain's representative in Vienna, began making plans to return to his military duties. No declaration of war was issued against France - in fact, Louis XVIII was a member of the alliance. The powers pledged not to lay down their arms until Napoleon had been crushed. All Europe was arrayed not against a country but against one man.

The campaign plan eventually agreed upon in Vienna shows how seriously the Allies were determined to defeat the usurper once and for all. It called for the careful maneuvering and close cooperation of six Allied armies. The Duke of Wellington, commanding a joint British, Dutch, and Belgian army of 95,000 men, would advance from the extreme north; slightly southeast of him would be 124,000 Prussians, led by Field Marshal Blücher. A third army of 200,000 Russians would enter France through the Saar. Schwarzenberg, the supreme commander, would bring 210,000 Austrian troops from the direction of Basel, Switzerland.

These four forces, a total of 629,000 men, would march on Paris by converging routes. Meanwhile, two smaller armies, provided by Austria and Sardinia, 75,000 troops in all, would cross the Alps from Italy and fan out across southern France to operate in conjunction with Britain's Mediterranean fleet. The Austrians and Russians had the greatest distances to cover. To allow them enough time to reach the agreed rendezvous, Schwarzenberg proposed that their invasion begin on June 27. In order to operate effectively with their allies farther south, the British and Prussians, who were closer, would wait until July 1 to cross the French frontier. By the end of June, the Allies would have massed well over 700,000 men on the French border.

To face this host, whose plans he could only guess at but whose numbers he could estimate quite accurately, Napoleon had only 200,000 men who were fit for combat. A large proportion of them would be needed to man his many frontier garrisons, leaving him only a small striking force. With the wisdom of hindsight, later historians have questioned Napoleon's sanity in hoping to defend himself successfully against an enemy four times stronger than he. But Napoleon was not only making a last, desperate gamble for power - he had reason to believe that he might accomplish a miracle and win.

Napoleon had defeated superior coalitions before. It would take quite a while before the Allied armies were ready to march, and the movements of large bodies of men over considerable distances always meant difficulties with supplies and communications. Language problems and mutual distrust among nationalities would certainly add to poor coordination on the part of the Allies. With luck, he would be able to pick them off one by one, and a single decisive victory might induce the other powers to negotiate peace. And, despite the Vienna declaration. Napoleon still hoped that war could be avoided, at least until he had time to get more men together to defend France.

But the powers refused to believe his announcement that he would abide by the treaty terms accepted by Louis XVIII in 1814. The various rulers to whom he sent personal assurances of his peaceful intentions returned his letters unopened. The Allies had many reasons not to trust Napoleon. Their chief fear was that, under his rule, France would never be content to accept a place as just another European power. Sooner or later, and probably sooner, the Emperor of the French would want to regain his former conquests. He would destroy the order and balance in Europe that they were trying so painfully to construct at Vienna.

Napoleon's actions after his return to Paris gave some substance to their fear. Power, he realized, must be based on the support of the people. All his actions in April and May were calculated to regain his popularity with the lower and middle classes. He amended his former imperial constitution to guarantee a degree of personal liberty and to establish at least the outward form of parliamentary government. He even armed several thousand volunteers from the workingmen's districts of Paris and Lyons. Perhaps, if he had risked identifying himself totally with the revolution, he might have rallied the bulk of the nation to his cause. For this, however, he was too cautious; he, too, was afraid of the masses.

As it happened, the response to his appeals was disappointing. Nobody had strongly opposed his return to power, but this was due more to apathy than to enthusiasm for his cause. When he asked the nation to ratify the new constitution, only a fraction of the voters bothered to go to the polls.

In his urgent need for troops, Napoleon ordered all those men who had been under arms in April 1814 and had technically never been demobilized to report for active duty. But the majority, hating conscription and resentful of the legal trick Napoleon had found to get around it, simply ignored his call. The militia, or National Guard, was equally unenthusiastic in its response. Only about 15,000 Frenchmen enlisted as volunteers. A number of his marshals and generals found excuses for not returning to active service.

France was tired of war, and unless Napoleon won a quick victory, he could count on no one's loyalty.

Thanks to his extraordinary energy, however, Napoleon succeeded in raising enough additional troops in two months to bring his total army strength to around 300,000 men. By June, he was able to concentrate 124,000 of them near the Belgian border, ready to take the offensive if need be. In addition, he had managed to equip the new army. The Paris workshops alone produced more than 1,200 uniforms each day. In two months, 12 million cartridges were manufactured. Twenty thousand muskets were being produced each month, and thousands more were repaired and made fit for service. In a word, Napoleon wasted no time.

Fortunately for his chances of success, the rest of Europe lacked the impetus of a single, energetic commander. The Russian forces, stationed close to their own frontier, had the farthest distance to cover and were very slow to get on the move. The Austrian army found itself unexpectedly engaged in a war against the only one of Napoleon's relations who had kept his throne, Joachim Murat, King of Naples.

On March 31, Murat issued a manifesto proclaiming himself king of all Italy. He may even have intended to come to the aid of his brother-in-law though he did not consult Napoleon in advance about his move. Austria and Britain, convinced that Murat was, indeed, the French emperor's ally, declared war on him immediately. It seems more likely, however, that the king of Naples was probably hoping to consolidate his own rather shaky position while the Allies' backs were turned. Murat's early successes diverted more and more Austrian troops into Italy until finally, early in May, they crushed his forces completely, and the defeated king sought refuge in France. Napoleon, whose one hope for an alliance had been thrown away by Murat's poor timing, angrily rejected his old comrade's offer to fight with him once again. He thereby lost the services of the best cavalry commander in Europe.

With the Russian army still far away and the Austrians occupied in Italy, the Allied forces closest to the French border were the British and Dutch-Belgian troops, concentrated in and around Brussels, and the Prussians, who had a garrison of about 60,000 men guarding the Rhine. After a nonstop journey from Vienna, the Duke of Wellington arrived in Brussels on April 4. To his dismay, he found that the Anglo-Dutch forces he was to command were a scant 33,000 instead of the large army he had expected. He surveyed the defenses and wrote immediately to the Prussian chief of staff, General August Neidhardt von Gneisenau. The Prussians, Wellington suggested, should begin to mass in southeast Belgium, between Charleroi and Liège, on the left of the sparsely-held British front. Only vague reports of Napoleon's movements were available, but it seemed obvious that together the British and Prussians stood a better chance of resisting a sudden thrust across the border, thirty-five miles from Brussels. On April 19, Blücher arrived in Liège from Berlin, and the two commanders began to build up their armies with all possible speed.

"I have an infamous army," Wellington complained to a friend early in May, "very weak and ill-equipped, and a very inexperienced staff. In my opinion they are doing nothing in England . . ." Despite his continual prodding, reinforcements were slow in coming. The Dutch-Belgian forces, Wellington felt, were of doubtful loyalty. Only the year before, many of them had been fighting under Napoleon's command. In addition, most of his seasoned British veterans from the six-year-long Peninsular campaign had been sent to the United States to fight Americans in the War of 1812. The fighting ended in January 1815, but the embarkation of troops took time, and numbers of Wellington's best men were still on the other side of the Atlantic. Gradually, however, he was able to recruit steady, experienced battalions from home to stiffen his green troops.

By the middle of June, Wellington's forces were quadrupled: he had 32,000 British troops, 32,000 Dutch-Belgians, and 29,000 Hanoverians and other German auxiliaries (affiliated with the British because King George III was also ruler of Hanover) - in all, some 93,000 men.

As for Blücher, Napoleon's levies had so emptied Prussia's treasury that the bulk of his troops had been demobilized in 1814 for lack of money to pay them. Volunteers now flocked to the standard, eager to fight against Napoleon. Outdoor recruiting posts were set up in Berlin, and young lads in their teens stood in line for hours to enlist. Raw and untrained though they were, these recruits were sturdy, full of patriotism, and longing to take vengeance on the French who had tried to bring their beloved country to her knees. Between April and June, the Prussian army in Belgium doubled in size, to about 120,000 men.

In mid-June 1815, the Allies had concentrated 213,000 troops in Belgium, ready to march against Napoleon at the end of the month. To face them, the emperor had an army little over half as large. But Napoleon's 124,000 men were the best he had had since Austerlitz - almost all were experienced soldiers, and almost all were Frenchmen, loyal to his cause. The only foreigners were several units of Polish lancers, whose fanatical devotion to Napoleon rivaled that of the stalwart veterans of his Old Guard. In contrast, the Allied forces were badly coordinated and poorly trained, and their respective leaders were temperamentally as ill-assorted as it is possible to imagine.

Arthur Wellesley - who had risen through every rank of the English peerage to become in 1814, at the age of forty-five, Duke of Wellington - was born in the same year as Napoleon. Although he was a gifted musician (he was a good amateur violinist), he showed no special aptitude for any other profession. Like many other younger sons of aristocratic families, he chose the army as his career; like most of his brother officers, he had gained his early steps in rank by buying his commissions. Unlike them, however, he took the trouble to learn his profession thoroughly.

In 1796, young Wellesley was sent to India, where he emerged as a remarkably successful commander. Five years of campaigning against the native princes who threatened the power of the British East India Company brought him several impressive victories and recognition as a promising young general. Later, in Portugal and in Spain, he proved himself as a tactician when he fought and defeated one after another of Napoleon's marshals in the Peninsular War. Yet he had never taken the field against Napoleon himself, and he had never commanded very large bodies of troops. His special talent was for defensive tactics and for the detailed planning and organization that can often win battles. He showed little interest in the larger concepts of warfare, and sudden masterly strokes of genius were no part of his character. Cold, arrogant, and fearless, Wellington was as contemptuous of death as he was of most of his subordinate officers and other ranks. No one ever contended that he was loved by his troops, but they would carry out almost superhuman assignments for him.

Gebhard Leberecht von Blücher, created Prince of Wahlstatt in 1813, was a man who had almost nothing in common with the cool, reserved Wellington. Seventy-two in 1815, he had survived a lifetime of hard drinking and other excesses without losing any of his extraordinary physical stamina or his hotheadedness. He served in the Seven Years' War under Frederick the Great of Prussia, but the eighteenth century's most-respected military expert thought little of his ability. When in 1773, Blücher resigned from the service on the grounds that he had been passed over for promotion, Frederick jotted on his application: "Captain Blücher may take himself to the Devil." Blücher in fact married and settled down on his estates for fifteen years to play the part of a rough-hewn country gentleman.

After Frederick's death, he resumed his army career, and in 1794, he became a major general. Blücher distinguished himself for courage and endurance in the disastrous Prussian campaign of 1806, but his rise was due more to his prominence in the anti-French party than to his intelligence. Like Wellington, he had entered the army as the younger son of an aristocratic family, for whom no further education was felt to be necessary. Unlike the British general, however, he understood little of war and strategy - indeed, he was almost illiterate. He was also subject to mental disturbances, in one of which he imagined that Napoleon had bribed his servants to heat the floor of his room to such a pitch that he would burn his feet, so he could be seen either sitting with his legs in the air or jumping around the room on the tips of his toes. It was while Blücher was in the grip of a delusion that he was about to give birth to an elephant that the chief of staff, General Gerhard von Scharnhorst, picked him as the ideal man to lead the army: "[Blücher] must lead though he have a hundred elephants inside of him," Scharnhorst wrote compellingly.

As it turned out, Scharnhorst was right. Despite his bluff and crude exterior, Blücher possessed several qualities that, at critical times, are invaluable in a chief. He never flinched from risk; he always preferred direct, aggressive action to caution; he never admitted defeat; and he was capable of recovering from stunning reverses almost immediately. Plus, he was adored by his troops. When in doubt whether to retreat or to attack, Blücher believed that attacking was always preferable. His men affectionately nicknamed him Marschall Vorwärts, "Marshal Forward."

Blücher and Wellington met twice during May. The Prussian field marshal, in common with most of his fellow countrymen, had an inbred hatred of the French and was eager to move against Napoleon right away. Wellington was as eager as any man to beat Napoleon, but unlike hotheaded old Blücher, the British commander was resigned to remaining on the defensive until the other Allied armies were fully ready. They agreed that if Napoleon should attack Wellington, Blücher would come to his assistance. The possibility that the reverse might happen - that is, that Napoleon might attack Blücher - does not seem to have occurred to Wellington.

In fact, both commanders were quite in the dark about Napoleon's intentions. There were two possibilities: Either Napoleon would attack the British and Prussian armies in Belgium or he would remain on the defensive in France and save his strength for a blow against Schwarzenberg's Austrian army, advancing from the east.

If Napoleon attacked to the north, Wellington felt that his main duty was the defense of Brussels and the protection of Ghent where Louis XVIII and his government had taken refuge. He must also keep open his lines of supply and communication - and, if necessary, retreat - to the Channel. What the duke feared most was a French offensive through northern Belgium that would cut him off from the sea and threaten Ghent. Consequently, he stationed his British and Dutch-Belgian units in widely-scattered positions, ready to concentrate anywhere within what he considered the most likely area for an attack.

Actually, Wellington did not expect an attack. The letters he wrote in May and early June clearly show that he regarded Napoleon's preparations on the other side of the frontier as purely defensive. The emperor's feints and ruses had thoroughly succeeded in deceiving his opponents.

Napoleon's general plan for the campaign he was about to launch had the simplicity of genius. The Anglo-Dutch forces were strung out in the north of Belgium between Ghent and Charleroi; the Prussians were grouped along the Sambre and Meuse valleys between Charleroi and Liège. Napoleon planned to rush his army to the weakest spot, the Charleroi area where the Allied commands should have overlapped but did not. He would use his men as a wedge to separate the enemy's two armies. Then he would strike at one of them, defeat it before the other could come to its assistance, and finally deal with the remaining army. The success of the operation depended not on numbers but on speed, surprise, and efficiency.

On June 6, in complete secrecy, Napoleon's army began to assemble near the Belgian border. To mislead the Allies about his intentions, the emperor - still in Paris - directed his men to build fortifications as if they expected to stay on the defensive. At 3:30 a.m. on June 12, in excellent spirits after a farewell dinner with his family, Napoleon left the capital in his carriage. By June 14, he had covered the 125 miles to his headquarters at Beaumont on the Belgian frontier. His army was ready to march, and Napoleon ordered operations to begin the next morning. In his Order of the Day for June 15, he reminded his army that the day was the anniversary of two of his greatest victories - that of Marengo in Italy, in 1800, and of Friedland, in the Prussian campaign of 1807. "The moment has come," the order ended, "to conquer or to perish."

The march across the frontier began while it was still dark. A thick morning mist covered the wooded hills and fertile valleys, but it soon lifted. The French encountered advanced units of General Hans Ernst Karl Graf von Zieten's First Prussian Corps stationed between Charleroi and the border, but these they easily pushed before them. By noon, Napoleon was riding into Charleroi under a brilliant sun. The citizens lined the streets, cheering enthusiastically. The emperor halted at an inn, had a chair brought outside, and sat watching his troops as they marched by, shouting "*Vive l'Empereur!*" Exhausted from nine hours in the saddle, he soon fell fast asleep in the hot sunshine.

Napoleon had well earned his rest. He had taken Wellington and Blücher completely by surprise. Judging from reports later given by officers and soldiers alike, the buildup of Wellington's forces was a chaos of inefficiency. The troops were scattered all over the country. Artillery units, for instance, were billeted miles away both from their gun parks and from the horse troops to which they were attached.

When the alert was finally given, many units were unable to arrive in time for the fighting. Most of the British officers regarded being on duty in Belgium as a chance to have a good time and do some sightseeing. Fashionable English families, especially those with marriageable daughters, had crowded into Brussels that spring, and the many officers who had formed part of aristocratic London society found themselves active as escorts at almost nightly balls. Life passed in a constant round of galas, parties, and outdoor entertainments.

No one thought Napoleon would strike so soon. Three days before the French marched upon Charleroi, the duke himself escorted Lady Jane Lennox, one of the pretty daughters of his friend the Duke of Richmond, to a cricket match at Enghien, thirty miles from Napoleon's headquarters at Beaumont. The evening of June 14, the duke spent romping with the Richmonds' younger children in Brussels; no message reached him from the frontier.

Blücher's headquarters was at Namur, closer to the border than Brussels. The Prussian commander was less nonchalant when, on June 14, he was told of the French troop concentration across the frontier. In fact, his reaction was foolhardy in the extreme. Blücher was not called Marshal Forward for nothing. He immediately ordered three of his four corps to concentrate at Sombreffe, within striking distance of the French. And he failed to notify his fellow commander of his movements to make sure that Wellington could come to his assistance. When Napoleon heard of his opponent's incredibly rash move, he at first refused to believe it. It was too good to be true.

4
CONFUSION AT THE CROSSROADS

June 15, 1815, was a day that began with an act of treason, continued with a series of mistakes, and ended with a brilliant ball.

Treason was committed by General Louis de Bourmont, one of Napoleon's division commanders, who had come over to the emperor's side with Marshal Ney at Auxerre. Unlike Ney, however, Bourmont was a royalist of long standing who had for years been bitterly opposed to Napoleon. The advance into Belgium gave him a chance to strike a blow for his old cause. With his staff, he rode off to surrender to the First Prussian Corps and reveal the emperor's campaign plan to General von Zieten. The general immediately sent on the information to Blücher at Namur, but the aged field marshal's rash reaction in effect canceled out Bourmont's treason.

Confident that he could resist Napoleon's entire army, Blücher confirmed his previous orders to concentrate at Sombreffe where he himself arrived at four in the afternoon. He finally sent word of his dispositions to Wellington at Brussels but failed to tell the British commander what route Napoleon was taking. This was the first blunder.

Meanwhile, at Charleroi, Napoleon was joined by Marshal Ney, whom he had ordered there from Paris. Napoleon had hesitated before employing Ney, whom he thought unreliable. Indeed, he had once complained that Ney was less able to understand his plans than was the youngest drummer boy in his army. But the marshal had been with Napoleon since his earliest campaigns. When it came to leading or rallying his men in battle, Ney was magnificent; he knew no fear and had a gift for inspiring men. His eager, excitable nature, however, made him apt to act rashly without weighing the significance of a military situation. The emperor's decision to give Ney command of the left wing of his army was probably a blunder, too - yet he had little choice, since most of his best commanders had refused to join him.

Napoleon had always kept his plans to himself. He never told his subordinates the reason behind the actions he assigned to them, which enabled him to keep tight personal control over his battles. His present instructions to Ney were verbal, and no record of them exists; no doubt Ney was ordered to proceed along the Charleroi-Brussels road. Whether he was also ordered to seize the vital crossroads at Quatre Bras, some eleven miles north of Charleroi before Wellington had time to concentrate his forces there remains a matter of argument. What actually happened was that Ney halted his infantry before nightfall at Gosselies, barely one-third of the way to the crossroads. This turned out the next day to have been a serious mistake.

As for his right wing, Napoleon entrusted it to Emmanuel de Grouchy, whom he had made a marshal for his service in putting down a brief royalist rebellion when the emperor returned from Elba. Though he now held the highest rank in the French army and had considerable experience as a cavalryman, Grouchy had never before held a field command. Napoleon instructed him to push Zieten's Prussians northeast to Sombreffe. But the emperor had failed to inform the right-wing generals of Grouchy's new status, and they refused to accept his orders. In fact, they spent so long bickering over the method of attack that the emperor himself had to ride out from Charleroi to spur them on. Zieten's own orders from Blücher were to fall back on Fleurus if he was attacked by superior forces, and he obeyed them to the letter.

Having finally set his right wing in pursuit of the Prussians, Napoleon returned to Charleroi to spend the night. His plans for the following day, June 16, were not quite settled yet. His intention was almost certainly to push on to Brussels with the main section of his army and thus to separate Wellington from Blücher. The French, who had seen no significant bodies of Wellington's troops, believed the Prussians to be retreating. There was no reason for the emperor to think that the French, on the morrow, would have to fight not one but two engagements. His day had begun before three o'clock that morning, and around nine that night, exhausted but unworried, he retired.

About thirty miles away in Brussels, the main event of the day was in progress - the grand ball given by the Duchess of Richmond, one of the leading British hostesses in Brussels. Earlier that month, she had asked Wellington, who was a personal friend, if she should give her ball in view of the rumors that the French were massing for an attack. "Duchess, you may give your ball with the greatest safety, without fear of interruption," replied the duke, who had himself issued invitations for a splendid function to be held a few days afterward. It seems almost inconceivable that Wellington did not cancel the now-famous ball since he had finally received word from Zieten earlier that afternoon that Napoleon's army had crossed the frontier.

It was the Duke of Wellington's fixed notion that the attack would come by way of Mons in order to turn his flank and cut him off from the sea. About 5:00 p.m., therefore, Wellington had issued orders to regroup his forces to the southwest of Brussels, safeguarding the Brussels-Mons road. If these commands had been carried out by Wellington's army, Napoleon could have annihilated Blücher the next day while Wellington's forces were seeking the French all over southwest Belgium. Fortunately for Wellington, two of his subordinate generals ignored his orders.

Late in the afternoon of June 15, Prince Carl Bernhard of Saxe-Weimar, who commanded a brigade in Wellington's army, came riding up to Quatre Bras with his 4,000 foot-soldiers and eight guns. Finding the crossroads unoccupied, he decided to stay there. He had heard that the French were at Charleroi, and it seemed elementary to him to deny them so strategic a place as Quatre Bras.

Shortly afterward, a French cavalry detachment of some 1,700 horsemen trotted along the road from the south to reconnoiter. To give the French an impression of strength, Prince Bernhard ordered his eight guns to let loose, and the cavalry commander sent back to Ney for infantry support. Instead, Ney himself rode up to survey the scene. The rye in the fields stood as high as a man, so he could not tell how large an enemy force he was facing. But he knew of Wellington's reputation for hiding the bulk of his troops to deceive his foes into attacking unwisely. He could also hear gunfire behind him, to the southeast, where Napoleon was attacking the Prussians, and he did not want to take the left wing too far in advance of the main body of his army. For once in his life, the marshal acted with caution. He withdrew his skirmishers and ordered his men to camp for the night at Gosselies.

At this point, the Duke of Wellington's order to concentrate in the direction of Mons reached Braine-le-Comte, headquarters of Willem Frederik George Lodewijk, the Prince of Orange, who commanded the Anglo-Dutch First Corps to which Bernhard was attached. The Prince of Orange, like almost everybody else of note, was away in Brussels, dancing at the Richmonds' ball; and his quartermaster general, Baron Jean de Constant Rebecque, was in command in his absence. Fortunately for Wellington, Rebecque was an experienced general who realized it would be absurd to obey an order to withdraw his troops from an area where he was in actual contact with the French. He and his subordinate commander, General Hendrik George de Perponcher, decided not only to ignore the order but to send another brigade to reinforce Bernhard at Quatre Bras. When he came back from the ball, the Prince of Orange backed their decision. Without their good judgment, Wellington would have lost Brussels.

About ten o'clock that night, Baron Karl von Muffling, the Prussian liaison officer at British headquarters in Brussels, brought the duke a message from General von Gneisenau, Blücher's chief of staff. The general informed Wellington that the Prussians were concentrating their troops at Sombreffe and expected to give battle the next day. What were their allies' intentions? Wellington, who was in his shirt sleeves, dressing for the Duchess of Richmond's ball, told Muffling that he could not give him this information until he had news from Mons. Since Gneisenau's message made no mention of the French having taken Charleroi in strength, there seemed no reason why Napoleon should not be planning a double attack upon the Allies. Still convinced that Mons was his weak point, the duke confirmed his earlier orders to cover the roads leading to Brussels from the southwest. In addition, he ordered the 20,000 men of the reserve billeted in and around the capital itself to be ready to move at any moment.

Not too long afterward, the eagerly-awaited dispatch from the commandant of the Mons garrison arrived. Any man but Wellington might have been unnerved by the news it contained: no Frenchmen were to be seen anywhere near Mons; Napoleon's entire army had taken the route to Charleroi. But the duke, as always, kept his composure. He canceled his previous orders and ordered all his commanders to march on Quatre

Bras. Toward midnight, he rejoined Muffling, saying briskly that he had given orders for his entire army to concentrate on Nivelles and Quatre Bras. Meanwhile, he and the baron would put in an appearance at the ball in order to make Napoleon's many friends in the city believe that the British were being taken by surprise.

The gathering, held in the rose-papered ballroom of the house the Richmonds had rented for the season, was brilliant, indeed. Elegant soldiers and diplomats mingled with the most beautiful women in Brussels. The ladies' dresses competed with their partners' colorful uniforms under the glittering crystal chandeliers. There were as many rumors as guests at the ball, and most of the senior officers present had been warned to leave early. But the laughing, chattering crowd did not seem in the least aware that Napoleon had already launched his attack. Three days later, half of the officers dancing that night would be dead or wounded in the struggle that decided the fate of Europe.

The duke arrived at the ball just before midnight. Lady Georgiana Lennox, Lady Jane's sister, came up to him to ask if the rumors were true. "Yes," he told her gravely, "we are off tomorrow." Lady Georgiana later wrote, "This terrible news was circulated directly, and while some of the officers hurried away, others remained at the ball, and actually had not time to change their clothes, but fought in evening costume. I went with my eldest brother [aide-de-camp to the Prince of Orange] . . . to help him pack up, after which we returned to the ballroom where we found some energetic and heartless young ladies still dancing. . . ."

Another guest, who shared a sofa with the duke, remarked afterward that although he "affected great gaiety and cheerfulness, it struck me that I had never seen him have such an expression of care and anxiety on his countenance." While chatting with her, Wellington kept breaking off in midsentence to give instructions to the aides-de-camp who hurried in and out with dispatches. At his suggestion, the Prince of Orange and the Duke of Brunswick left to return to their commands just as the guests sat down to supper.

Shortly afterward, Wellington quietly asked the Duke of Richmond if he had a good map of the region. "Yes," said his host and led him to the adjacent dressing room he used as a study. Wellington shut the door and exclaimed, "Napoleon has humbugged me, by God! He has gained twenty-four hours on me!" The Duke of Richmond asked, "What do you intend doing?" Wellington replied, "I have ordered the army to concentrate at Quatre Bras. But we shan't stop him there, and if so, we must fight him *here*."

As Wellington spoke, he passed his thumbnail over the map, and Richmond made a pencil line below the name of the little village he indicated: Waterloo.

At midnight, just about the time Wellington was changing his orders, Marshal Ney arrived at the inn in Charleroi where Napoleon was sleeping. The emperor was wakened, and they had supper together. For two hours they talked - but again, nobody knows whether or not Napoleon gave Ney definite orders to take Quatre Bras. About two o'clock in the morning of June 16, the emperor went back to sleep (he had always possessed the talent of sleeping at will, in any situation). At four, he rose again and began to issue orders for the coming operations. Unaware of the Prussian concentration at Sombreffe, he was still planning to make his main thrust against Wellington in Brussels. However, Napoleon had to make sure that the Prussians would be unable to link up with Wellington's forces. He ordered his right wing, under Marshal Grouchy, to push Zieten's corps back beyond Gembloux, thus gaining control of the Namur-Brussels road. Once this had been done, Napoleon himself with the reserves would join his left wing (that is, Ney's forces) and march upon the capital by the Charleroi-Brussels route.

In his instructions to Ney, he explained this plan and ordered him to detach one division to join Grouchy, to hold six more divisions at Quatre Bras, and to send an eighth division to occupy Genappe, two miles to the north of Quatre Bras, on the road to Brussels. In all these dispositions, Napoleon did only what common sense dictated. Since the three sections of his army - left wing, right wing, and reserve - were only a few miles apart, they could come to one another's assistance as circumstances dictated, even if there was a change of plan.

That there had to be a change of plan occurred to Napoleon as early as 8:00 a.m. on June 16. At that hour, an aide-de-camp dispatched by Marshal Grouchy informed the emperor that the whole Prussian army seemed to be assembling around Sombreffe and that consequently he was hardly in a position to attack. At first, Napoleon refused to believe this, and to make sure, he decided to look for himself. Leaving the Sixth Corps under General Georges de Lobau with orders to guard Charleroi, he got on his horse and rode to Fleurus. By 11:00 a.m., he was surveying the scene from a convenient windmill. Before him, Blücher's entire army appeared to be taking up its positions. The sight filled Napoleon with joy. Instantly, he reversed his plans. He would attack and destroy the Prussian army that afternoon and then join Ney and deal with the British. To rout Blücher, however, he would need Ney's cooperation. His assumption (mistaken) was that Ney was already in possession of Quatre Bras and would be able, later in the afternoon, to bring up the bulk of his forces against the Prussians and thus make the victory complete.

About 2:00 p.m., Napoleon's chief of staff, Marshal Nicolas Soult, wrote Ney of the planned attack on Blücher, adding: "It is His Majesty's intention that you will also attack whatever force is in front of you [that is, Wellington's troops] and push it back vigorously; which done, you will turn in our direction, so as to bring about the envelopment of the body of the enemy's troops I have just mentioned to you [that is, Blücher's army]." Nothing, it seemed to Napoleon, could be clearer.

A few minutes before three, Napoleon gave the signal (three cannon shots fired at regular intervals) for the attack on the Prussian position, which was centered on the little village of Ligny. About half an hour later, since there was still no word from Ney, Napoleon sent a more urgent message to his marshal: "The fate of France is in your hands," Soult wrote at his dictation. "Thus do not hesitate even for a moment to carry out the maneuver." By this time, however, Ney was no longer able to carry out his instructions.

At ten that morning, Wellington had arrived with his staff at Quatre Bras, having left the ball at three and having slept a couple of hours (like Napoleon, he could cat nap whenever he chose). To his surprise, he found that Ney had still not attacked the crossroads. Even at that late hour, the French could easily have dislodged the Allies, for Wellington's forces, confused by the conflicting orders he had issued the night before, were slow in concentrating.

The British troops of the reserve began to arrive at Quatre Bras about midafternoon, many of them after a thirty-mile march. Officers arrived from Brussels on horseback or in cabs, some of them still dressed for the Duchess of Richmond's ball. Captain Cavalié Mercer of the British horse artillery recalled seeing "a cabriolet, driving at a smart pace," passing him as it neared the battlefield. "In it was seated an officer of the Guards, coat open and snuffbox in hand. I could not help but admire the perfect nonchalance with which my man was thus hurrying forward to join in a bloody combat - much, perhaps, in the same manner, though certainly not in the same costume, as he might drive to [the races at] Epsom or Ascot Heath."

That morning, Marshal Ney must have slept later than Napoleon had. It was only at eleven, after receiving the emperor's first set of orders, that he began to bestir himself. If Wellington had issued his order to concentrate at Quatre Bras a few hours earlier than the preceding midnight, the marshal's delay would have been fatal. Indeed, if Wellington had had enough men at Quatre Bras that morning, he could have veered off in Blücher's direction and done to Napoleon precisely what Napoleon hoped to do to Blücher - that is, catch him between two jaws. As it happened, thanks to the failure of both Ney and Wellington to grasp the situation, nothing at all took place at Quatre Bras on the morning of June 16. Shortly after eleven, since all seemed tranquil, Wellington decided to ride over to Blücher's headquarters, about eight miles to the east, to see what was going on there.

Wellington and Blücher met near Ligny about 1:00 p.m. and surveyed the area from the top of a windmill. Across the valley, they could see Napoleon's forces drawing up for the impending battle. Blücher, as usual, was optimistic. Wellington promised to come to his aid unless he himself were attacked at Quatre Bras and then criticized the disposition of Blücher's troops. The field marshal had placed his men on the forward slope of a hill. Wellington pointed out that it was his practice to conceal his troops behind a hill and to have them come up only after his artillery had prepared the attack. "My men prefer to see the enemy," said Blücher. Wellington did not insist, but after taking his leave he remarked, "If they fight here, they will be damnably mauled." He was quite right.

About 3:00 p.m., just as Napoleon began to attack the Prussians at Ligny, Wellington returned to Quatre Bras. There he found a furious struggle going on. Ney had attacked at last. But - bravest of the brave though he was - Ney was still acting with unusual caution because he suspected Wellington's troops were more numerous than they appeared to be. As Wellington had just been telling Blücher, it was his habit to conceal the bulk of his forces. A thorough reconnaissance would have made plain to Ney that on this occasion, the duke had no forces to conceal. Instead of sending out patrols, however, he ordered an extremely cautious attack. This gave Wellington the time he needed to build up his strength, and by four o'clock, his troops outnumbered those of General Honoré Reille, whom Ney had charged with the task of capturing the crossroads.

It must be said in Ney's defense that since Napoleon's two-o'clock message had not yet arrived, Ney still had no idea that Napoleon had come upon Blücher's army and had decided to direct his main effort against it. The marshal, therefore, could not know how important it was to take Quatre Bras speedily. In fact, he was still relying on Napoleon to come to his aid, while Napoleon was counting on *him* to decide the battle at Ligny. Nobody had expected that there would be two battles that day a few miles' distance from each other.

If the chief commanders were confused, lesser mortals were absolutely bewildered. While the battle was raging at Quatre Bras, Captain Mercer was trying to make his way toward it over roads clogged with wounded, deserters, and baggage trains. He did not reach the battle in time to be of use, but he had the observant eye of an artist, and he left an account of what he saw. His unit had just emerged from a forest and was approaching the town of Nivelles, about six miles west of the scene of battle, when he "became sensible of a dull, sullen sound that filled the air, somewhat resembling that of a distant watermill, or still-more-distant thunder. . . . The increasing intensity of the cannonade, the volumes of smoke about the trees, led us to suppose the battle near at hand."

In Nivelles, they found the whole population in the streets, "huddled together in little groups like frightened sheep" or "hurrying along with the distracted air of people uncertain where they are going or what they are doing." The wounded were beginning to pour in from the battlefield. "Some were staggering along unaided, the blood falling from them in large drops as they went. . . . Priests were running to and fro, hastening to assist at the last moments of a dying man; all were in haste - all wore that abstracted look so inseparable from those engaged in an absorbing pursuit."

Leaving these scenes behind, Mercer and his men continued toward Quatre Bras. They found the road filled with soldiers going in the opposite direction, many of them wounded. But the number of unwounded men running away from the battle struck him as truly extraordinary. Most of them, it would seem, were Belgian recruits who sympathized with the French and had no desire to let themselves be killed in the service of the King of Holland. As he came closer to the battlefield, Mercer passed taverns filled with soldiers, "some standing about in earnest conversation, others seated round tables, smoking, carousing, and thumping the boards with clenched fists. . . ."

Captain Mercer was confused. Was he in a battle or was he not? Was the battle finished or still going on, and who was winning? Since cannon balls and shells were flying overhead, he decided that he *was* in a battle - but his guns never fired a shot in it. And even today, the argument continues over who actually won the battle of Quatre Bras.

At Ligny, on the right wing, Napoleon did not even realize that anything more than a skirmish was going on at Quatre Bras. Just after he had sent Ney the second message telling the marshal that the fate of France was in his hands, he himself received a dispatch from General Lobau who was still in Charleroi. According to Lobau, Ney was battling it out with an enemy 20,000 strong. This message should have reminded Napoleon that the 10,000 men of Lobau's Sixth Corps had been left at Charleroi where they were helping neither Ney nor the emperor's army. But he sent them no orders, and Lobau's corps remained where it was, doing nothing.

The emperor knew by now that Ney could not come

to Ligny to help him destroy the Prussians, but he was still convinced that the marshal could hold his own without additional troops. Consequently, he sent a hastily-scribbled order to General Drouet d'Erlon, whose First Corps was on its way from Gosselies to join Ney at Quatre Bras. This directed the general, whose 20,000 men formed part of Ney's left wing, to turn east and march to join Napoleon at Ligny instead.

The battle at Ligny, by that time, had turned into bloody hand-to-hand fighting. The French had started the attack with bands playing and banners waving, and the Prussians responded with murderous artillery and musket fire. The French advance was slowed down by ferocious resistance and counterattacks, and each street had to be taken house by house. By about 5:00 p.m., however, Blücher's men, most of them new and inexperienced troops, were at the end of their strength. Moreover, one of his four corps - the one commanded by General Friedrich Wilhelm von Bülow - had become lost while marching to join him and never reached the battle at all. Lacking Bülow's 30,000 men, Blücher had to commit his last reserves.

This was the moment Napoleon had been waiting for. Now, with the help of Ney's or d'Erlon's men, he could deliver the decisive blow to Blücher. But there was no trace of Ney nor of d'Erlon. The emperor had the choice of waiting for them or sending in his Guard. It was his policy never to commit the Guard - his most experienced troops - unless it was absolutely necessary. He decided to wait. Meanwhile, he dispatched a staff officer, Major Baudus, with a verbal message for Ney.

While Napoleon had been waiting for d'Erlon's corps at Ligny, Ney had been waiting for it at Quatre Bras. The British and Brunswicker troops under Wellington had put up an incredibly stubborn resistance aided by constant dribbles of reinforcements. At 4:00 p.m., the crossroads was still in their hands. To make another push, Ney counted on d'Erlon's 20,000 fresh troops coming up from the rear. They were practically within sight of Quatre Bras when Napoleon's aide overtook them and delivered the emperor's order to turn to Ligny. The note was scrawled in pencil, and d'Erlon misread the directions. Obediently, he ordered his corps to wheel to the right and marched them off toward Ligny - though not by the route that Napoleon expected. Then, recollecting his duty toward Ney, he sent his chief of staff to tell the marshal what had happened.

When Ney heard that the emperor had taken away his vital reserves, he turned livid with rage. Before his anger had even reached its peak, an aide galloped up with Marshal Soult's dispatch telling him that the fate of France was in his hands. From

Ney's point of view, Napoleon was deliberately making it impossible for him to beat Wellington at Quatre Bras. Furious, and as impulsive as ever, he sent a messenger after d'Erlon's corps with strict orders to turn back and rejoin the left wing. In doing this, he did not stop to think that, by the time d'Erlon's men returned, it would probably be too late for them to be useful. It was fast becoming clear to Ney that Wellington's forces were building up to major strength, and he decided on a desperate blow with all the forces at his disposition.

Ney called his cavalry commander, General François Étienne Kellermann, whose heavy cavalry was still in reserve. "The fate of France is in your hands," Ney told him, repeating Napoleon's phrase. Kellermann's cavalry must charge the Allied infantry and wipe them out. Kellermann was a brave commander who had never questioned an order in his life. Realizing that his superior had lost his judgment in his rage, he pointed out that three of his four cavalry brigades had been left in the rear and that he could hardly expect to overrun 25,000 men with 800 cuirassiers. "What does that matter?" Ney shouted at him. "Charge with whatever you've got. Gallop over them. I'll support you with all the cavalry that I have on the spot. Off with you. I say, off with you!"

It was Kellermann's turn to lose his temper. If he was ordered to commit suicide - all right, he would do it. Impetuously, he ordered his brigade to form a column and to charge straight at the enemy lines. "I used great haste," he wrote after the battle, "so that my men would have no time to shirk or to see the full danger facing them." The trumpets sounded the call for the charge, with Kellermann, his sword drawn, riding twenty paces ahead of his squadrons. Helmets and breastplates shimmered in the heat as the steady trot became a furious gallop that shook the ground. Riding at breakneck speed, the French column crashed through the British 69th Regiment, which had not had time to form properly, killed its colonel, and captured its colors. Charging past the 30th and 33rd regiments, which had formed in squares, the brigade dashed up a slope, cut down the gunners of a battery, overran a square of Brunswickers, and halted, finally, at the crossroads of Quatre Bras.

The feat was astounding, but useless. It was only then that the cuirassiers had time to notice that they were surrounded by the enemy. Kellermann had acted with such speed that Ney had had no time to bring up his other cavalry or to throw in his infantry to support the tremendous charge. Fire rained in on them from all sides. Kellermann's horse was shot from under him. Despite all his attempts to rally them, the cuirassiers wheeled their horses and charged back in the direction from which they had come. As they reached their own lines, they carried several advancing French infantry battalions with them in their panic. Wellington, seeing the French in disorder, at once ordered his troops to advance.

At this moment, Major Baudus arrived at Ney's side to deliver his oral message from Napoleon: under no circumstances must the marshal countermand the emperor's orders to d'Erlon. The action at Quatre Bras was of secondary importance. It was Ligny that really mattered. If Ney could not help Napoleon there, he must limit himself to containing Wellington's men in his present position.

The marshal was now beside himself with rage. He screamed at Baudus that on no account would he countermand his orders to d'Erlon. Then he turned his back on the major and rushed into the disorderly crowd of infantry, scattered by their own cuirassiers and the subsequent British attack. Drawing his sword and shouting encouragement, Ney managed to rally his men and personally led them in one countercharge after another. On this, as on other such occasions, he was superb.

But by now, Wellington's forces had grown too large to be resisted. Slowly and in good order, the French fell back. By nightfall, when the fighting ceased, they were in exactly the same positions they had occupied at noon. Neither side held the advantage. The Anglo-Dutch casualties were at least 4,700, the French casualties only a few hundred less. More than 9,000 men had been lost in a battle that had gained nothing.

At Ligny, the afternoon was nearing its close in a nightmare of noise and flames. The entire village was on fire, and Frenchmen and Prussians stabbed and shot one another amid the screams of their wounded, who were trapped inside the burning ruins. At 5:30, just as he was readying the Guard for a final attack on the Prussian center, Napoleon received word that a strong enemy column was approaching from the direction of Fleurus. It seemed impossible that Wellington or Blüher could have turned the tables on him by attacking him from the rear; nevertheless, he halted the Guard. It soon turned out that the distant column must be d'Erlon's corps, which had taken the wrong route because of the emperor's poor handwriting. But instead of joining their comrades, d'Erlon's men disappeared again as mysteriously as they had appeared. Their commander had received Ney's order to return to Quatre Bras. Heaping one more blunder on top of the many committed that day, he decided, without even consulting or notifying the emperor, to obey Marshal Ney. Not until nine o'clock did his weary troops rejoin Ney's forces at Quatre Bras, where, by then, the fighting had ceased. Hungry and footsore, they had spent the whole day marching back and forth between two battles without firing a shot.

D'Erlon's appearance and disappearance had panicked the left flank of Napoleon's army at Ligny. One of the divisions fled and was driven back to its position only when its commander turned his artillery on his own men. Blücher tried to exploit this incident by launching a counterattack, but the French speedily halted it. At last, nearly two hours after he had originally intended, Napoleon ordered his Guard to throw their full weight into the battle.

This final attack was preceded by an intense cannonade. At the same time - about 7:30 - the black thunderheads that had been gathering in the sky all afternoon burst into a violent electric storm. It was impossible to distinguish the cannons from the thunder, and the cloudburst that followed soaked the powder in the soldiers' priming pans and made their muskets useless. Yet the Guard charged with their bayonets, shouting "*Vive l'Empereur!*" Several brigades of cavalry thundered after them, and the Prussian center collapsed under the furious onslaught.

As suddenly as it had started, the downpour ceased, and the slanting rays of the setting sun burst upon the battlefield. Although his center had been demolished, Blücher still refused to acknowledge defeat. At the head of only two brigades of cavalry, the seventy-two-year-old field marshal personally led a desperate attack on the Guard who formed in squares to repulse him. The

French cavalry counterattacked, and the clash of horsemen lasted until dusk.

This last phase of the battle was a scene of utter confusion. Blücher's horse was hit by a cannon ball and collapsed on top of the old man. Nobody noticed it except the field marshal's aide, Count Nostitz, who stopped to assist him. While Nostitz was trying to extricate Blücher, a squadron of French cuirassiers thundered past. A few minutes later, with Blücher still pinned under his horse, they came racing back under the impact of a Prussian countercharge. Neither time did they realize that the enemy commander in chief was at their mercy. At last, with the help of a few Prussian cavalrymen, Nostitz succeeded in dragging his chief to safety. Bruised and only semiconscious, the field marshal was lifted onto a trooper's horse, and the little group protecting him was swept away in the general flight of the Prussian center.

The Prussian right and left wings kept up resistance for some time longer and then began to fall back in an orderly retreat. Napoleon had won a victory but not the complete one he had hoped for. Blücher had lost 16,000 men killed and wounded (against 12,000 French casualties). His own whereabouts remained unknown for several hours, and during the night, some 8,000 Prussian troops from the Rhineland deserted and fled east in the direction of home.

Late that evening, the officers on Blücher's staff met in council by the roadside to decide where to direct the retreat. There was no news of Blücher, and the command fell to his second in command, General von Gneisenau, an exceptionally able man. Peering at a map of the area by the light of the moon, Gneisenau made his decision. Instead of retreating to the east toward Liège and Germany, along its lines of supply, the Prussian army would fall back on Wavre, in the north.

According to Wellington, "this was the decisive moment of the century." Indeed, it was the only truly brilliant decision made by any commander during that entire day. For Wavre is less than ten miles to the east of the village of Waterloo, where Wellington was intending to make his stand. Gneisenau knew nothing of Wellington's intentions. Yet, even if he had known them, he was not at that moment disposed to cooperate with the British forces.

Unaware of the action at Quatre Bras, he felt that Wellington had betrayed his promise to come to the aid of the Prussians at Ligny, and he did not trust the Englishman's cooperation in the future. It was not to please Wellington that Gneisenau chose Wavre, but because he realized that from there, he could operate in any direction that seemed convenient. To retreat to Namur and Liège would have meant that the Prussian army was defeated. To retreat to

Wavre meant that it had merely suffered a setback. Wellington was right: Gneisenau's choice was a decisive moment, and Gneisenau chose correctly.

Shortly afterward, Gneisenau came upon Blücher in the tiny village of Mellery. The field marshal was resting on a bed of straw, sipping milk, and though badly shaken, he was in good spirits. Apparently he had anticipated Gneisenau's decision, for Mellery was on the route to Wavre.

It is barely seven miles from Ligny to Quatre Bras. Yet not until 7:30 the next morning did one of Wellington's aides, sent to discover what had happened to the Prussians, come dashing back on a foam-covered horse to report their defeat. An hour or so later, a messenger arrived from Blücher and Gneisenau to tell the duke that they were concentrating their entire army on Wavre.

Until he heard this, Wellington had thought he was victorious. His forces still kept arriving from all over Belgium. Although he had not totally defeated Ney on June 16, he was confident of crushing him and Napoleon as well on the seventeenth, provided Blücher held out. The Prussian retreat meant that Wellington had to make fresh plans. His men spent the night on the battlefield, soaked by the storm, and his first orders were for them to light fires and get a hot meal. Then, for about an hour, he paced up and down by himself, deep in thought. He was carrying a small switch in his right hand and frequently put the end in his mouth, apparently unconscious that he was doing so. Finally, he stood still and turned to his staff.

"Old Blücher," he remarked, "has had a damned good licking and gone back to Wavre, eighteen miles. As he has gone back, we must go, too. I suppose in England they'll say we have been licked. Well, I can't help it. As they are gone back, we must go too."

Then he issued orders for his army to retreat and dispatched the Prussian messenger back to Wavre. He was to tell his commanding officers that Wellington was moving back to a point between Quatre Bras and Brussels. There, about twelve miles from the capital, he would engage Napoleon in battle, provided that the Prussians could send him one corps in support. Just thirty-two hours earlier, the duke had pointed out on the map in the Duke of Richmond's study the place where his army would make its stand. Its name was Waterloo.

5
THE SAVING STORM

A t eight in the evening of June 16, Napoleon
dictated a victory bulletin from his
headquarters at Fleurus. According to this,
he had completely defeated the *united* British and
Prussian armies and was about to follow them in
hot pursuit. This, of course, was a vast exaggeration,
if not an outright lie.

The victory had been by no means complete: The
British and Prussian armies had fought separately,
and Napoleon's delay in ordering the pursuit of
the Prussians was fatal. Yet the emperor knew
that the public in Paris had to hear good news. He
seemed just as worried about what was happening
there in his absence as he was concerned about his
current operations in the field. The news of a great

victory would have a heartening effect; since he felt completely confident of routing Wellington within the next forty-eight hours, he would speedily make good his boast. Napoleon had always made the mistake of despising the abilities both of the British troops and of their commander in chief.

The inhabitants of Brussels were awakened that night by a troop of Belgian cavalry that had fled from Quatre Bras. They galloped through the city, spreading panic as they went. Citizens bargained with one another for carriages, horses, wagons, canal boats - anything that would enable them to save themselves and their possessions from the ravages of the French army that was expected to descend on the city at any moment.

About noon on June 17, a long, steady stream of wounded began to pour into Brussels. Some arrived in the clumsy farm carts that were the only ambulances available; others had managed to drag themselves on foot from the battlefield. One eyewitness described "wounded soldiers lying on the pavement, having got as far as the town, but unable to crawl farther - the dismay was universal." The population of Brussels felt there could be little doubt that the Anglo-Dutch army had been routed.

To the officers and other ranks of the Prussian army in retreat, it seemed equally certain that Blücher had been defeated. Among them was Francis Lieber, a fifteen-year-old volunteer who kept a sketchy diary of the campaign. On June 16 and 17, 1815, he did not have time to make long entries in his diary. On June 16, all he wrote was "Battle at Flöry." [He meant Fleurus, the nearest town to Ligny.] The next day: "In full flight—bivouacked twice." Napoleon's victory would have been almost as complete as he claimed in his bulletin if there had not been at least two men who did not feel that they had been beaten. One was the Duke of Wellington, who went to sleep on June 16 with the idea that he had been victorious at Quatre Bras. The other was old Blücher, who could not deny that he had been mauled at Ligny, but who refused to admit that he had been "licked," as Wellington put it.

The reasons for Napoleon's inactivity after his victory at Ligny have puzzled historians at least as much as they puzzled his officers at the time. Instead of ordering a general pursuit of the retreating Prussians, Napoleon returned to his headquarters and went to bed. Marshal Grouchy, seeking instructions for the right wing he commanded, was told to come back in the morning. But when he returned at an early hour, the emperor was having breakfast, and the marshal had to wait in an antechamber. While Napoleon ate his meal, one of his aides-de-camp brought him a report from Ney, sent the night before, with news of what had happened at Quatre Bras. A little later, a message was received from General Claude Pajol who was commanding a small cavalry detachment ordered to pursue and observe the retreating Prussians. According to Pajol, the Prussians were in headlong flight in the direction of Liège. Actually, of course, the bulk of the Prussian army was retreating toward Wavre. The men Pajol had seen were the 8,000 Rhenish deserters, who were running home as fast as they could.

Napoleon did not question Pajol's report since it seemed natural to him that the defeated enemy would withdraw toward Liège. It is surprising that the emperor did not order an immediate pursuit. Perhaps he had lost his ability to grasp a situation quickly and to take immediate action. Or perhaps he did not wish to act until he had a clearer picture of the situation. The most plausible explanation seems to be that Napoleon regarded the Prussians as utterly defeated, and he could direct his attention to Wellington's army without bothering about Blücher at all. Even so, it was against his nature not to make sure of the facts before proceeding on such an assumption. The thought that he should make sure, however, occurred to him only several hours later.

At 8:30 a.m., the emperor emerged from his room, and Marshal Grouchy hoped that at last he would be told what to do. But Napoleon, instead of issuing orders, told the marshal to follow the imperial coach: Napoleon was going to inspect the battlefield and review his troops at Ligny. The coach jolted so vigorously - as Grouchy was to recall later - that Napoleon, who was not feeling well, decided to get out and continue on horseback. The marshal seized the chance to ask him for instructions but was immediately snubbed. "I will give you my orders when I think fit," the emperor said icily. Arriving at the battlefield, he inspected the troops, talked to the wounded, and discussed the political scene in Paris with his entourage. He did everything, in fact, except tell anyone what to do next.

He had, however, dictated instructions for Ney to Marshal Soult. But the instructions were so obscure that Ney totally failed to understand them. There are, of course, a number of English translations, yet they all disagree. It is easy to see why Ney misunderstood the message. Napoleon's order certainly lacked any sense of urgency, and only one thing in it was quite clear to the marshal: the emperor was very displeased with his conduct the day before.

This knowledge made Ney so angry he did not even try to understand the remaining - and far more important - part of his instructions that seemingly were contradictory. On the one hand, the message told him to keep his men together and spend the day regrouping them after the battle. On the other, it suggested that he should attack Quatre Bras if it was held only by a rear guard. If the British were present in force, he should inform Napoleon and await his arrival from Ligny.

At about eleven o'clock, Napoleon received a message Ney had dispatched at dawn informing him that the British forces were still in Quatre Bras and seemed likely to attack. The emperor suddenly seemed to wake up and become his old energetic self once more. Lobau's Sixth Corps, which had been inactive all this time, was ordered forward from Charleroi to rendezvous with the Imperial Guard close to Quatre Bras. A second message to Ney, sent at noon, ordered him to add these forces to his own and launch an attack on Wellington (whose troops, by that time, had started their retreat toward Waterloo). As for Marshal Grouchy, he received - and misinterpreted - the most important orders given that day.

Grouchy's instructions were written by General Henri Bertrand, Napoleon's Grand Marshal of the Palace, at the emperor's dictation, so there was no question of illegibility. But Napoleon must have forgotten that Grouchy, an unimaginative man, would take them literally. In fact, the marshal failed to understand their main intention, which was expressed in these lines: "It is important to discover what the enemy intends to do, whether Blücher is moving away from Wellington or whether he means to unite with him in order to cover Brussels and Liège and thus risk the outcome of another battle." All that Grouchy paid attention to was the obvious part of the order, which was to proceed to Gembloux with 28,000 infantry and 5,000 cavalry. This is exactly what Grouchy did, and when he reached Gembloux, he stayed there.

Grouchy can be blamed only for being unimaginative, literal-minded, and a little slow. Napoleon, however, had committed a tactical error in letting the Prussians withdraw without keeping in close touch with them. Apparently only at 11:30, when he sent the order to Grouchy, did it occur to Napoleon the Prussians might have retreated in some other direction than Liège and that they could be on their way to join Wellington. If Grouchy had shown intelligence and initiative, Napoleon's error could have been repaired. By the time the marshal and his men reached Gembloux, the retreating Prussians could not have been farther than about five miles to the northwest. Grouchy had 5,000 cavalrymen, and a twenty-minutes ride would have brought them in contact with the Prussians. But instead of taking steps on his own, Grouchy sent a messenger asking for fresh instructions from the emperor. He never received them.

Meanwhile, at Quatre Bras, Marshal Ney was also distinguishing himself by inaction. It is true that Napoleon's orders to him were not at all clear. Yet no matter how Ney interpreted them, he ought to have realized that Napoleon intended him to fall upon Wellington with all his forces. These, with the addition of d'Erlon's corps and other troops that had taken no part in the previous day's fighting, amounted to at least 40,000 men - quite enough to mount a formidable attack. But the marshal was uncertain about whether or not the emperor would support him with the reserve once he did attack. Conscious of Napoleon's reprimand for the earlier occasion when he had acted on his own, Ney let the hours pass without doing anything.

At 10:00 a.m., Wellington's army had begun its orderly retreat. The infantry moved off first, battalion by battalion, while a protective rear guard of riflemen and cavalry stayed in Quatre Bras, ready to repel a French attack. It never came. Ney let Wellington's entire army get away without even pursuing it. Nor did he inform Napoleon of what was happening.

The message Napoleon dictated at noon was an unmistakable order to attack Wellington. Had the duke still been at Quatre Bras when Ney received it, the marshal might have obeyed. Then Napoleon, coming from the east, could have caught the Anglo-Dutch army, as he had hoped, in a trap. A single blow at such a time might, indeed, have won the campaign. But the enemy had withdrawn, and Ney could not have attacked him now even if he had wanted to.

An hour after sending Ney his second order,

Napoleon reached Marbais, four miles southeast of Quatre Bras. He expected to hear the thunder of cannons, but to his surprise, there was absolute silence. Riding over to Quatre Bras, he found out that Ney had let the Anglo-Dutch army get away. "You have ruined France!" Napoleon cried.

Only one possible way was left to win a decisive victory. The French must catch up with Wellington and beat him before Blücher could re-form his army and march to the duke's aid. Suddenly Napoleon became all energy again. Ordering all his cavalry forward in pursuit of the enemy, he set an example of initiative by galloping ahead of them himself. First the troops of horse artillery, then the infantry battalions, gradually fell into place behind them. Soon Napoleon came upon Wellington's rear guard - the Earl of Uxbridge's cavalry that included Mercer's troop of horse artillery. Shells and cannon balls began to shower on the French, but the emperor continued to lead them forward, shouting to the French artillerymen to return the British fire.

Captain Mercer himself left an account of that amazing scene. "The sky," he wrote, "had become overcast since the morning, and at this moment presented a most extraordinary appearance. Large isolated masses of thunder cloud, of the deepest, almost-inky black . . . hung suspended over us, involving our position and everything on it in deep and gloomy obscurity; whilst the distant hill lately occupied by the French army still lay bathed in brilliant sunshine." Lord Uxbridge, Mercer continued, was giving commands to his officers when a single horseman - Napoleon - appeared against the skyline. Soon several others joined him, their dark figures outlined against the sunshine on the distant hill. "Lord Uxbridge cried out 'Fire! Fire!' and giving them a general discharge, we quickly limbered up to retire as they dashed forward, supported by some artillery guns which fired upon us. . . . The first gun that was fired seemed to burst the clouds overhead, for its report was instantly followed by an awful clap of thunder, and lightning that almost blinded us whilst the rain came down as if a waterspout had broken over us. The sublimity of the scene was inconceivable. Flash succeeded flash, and the peals of thunder were long and tremendous."

The French guns kept up a brisk fire, but they seemed almost inaudible compared to the thunder. At the same time, the French cavalry dashed forward, adding their shouts to the appalling noise. "We galloped for our lives through the storm," said Captain Mercer, "straining to gain the enclosures about the houses of the hamlets, Lord Uxbridge urging us on, crying, 'Make haste! - Make haste! For God's sake gallop, or you will be taken!'"

Thus began that famous thunderstorm that proved

Wellington's salvation and Napoleon's undoing. The roads and fields were quickly transformed into slithery quagmires. The horses of the rear guard kept slipping, and many a young British cavalry officer found his smart uniform plastered with mud from head to foot. But if the downpour caused the Anglo-Dutch troops bruised bones and muddy breeches, it did much more damage to the French, preventing them from keeping up a close pursuit. The fields became impassable, and the whole French column - cavalry, artillery, and infantry - had to march strung out along the narrow, muddy road, which the hoofs of the retreating horses had stamped into a morass. Nor was this a short downpour as it had been the day before when Napoleon's Guard had charged the Prussians at Ligny. The torrential rain poured down like a monsoon, almost without abating, all the rest of the afternoon and throughout the night. At first, it brought some relief from the sultry heat, but soon the soldiers of both armies were chilled to the bone.

By 6:30 p.m., the Anglo-Dutch rear guard had reached the position designated by Wellington in the morning - the heights just south of the village of Waterloo, on the Charleroi-Brussels road. The rain had momentarily stopped, and for the second time that day, Captain Mercer of the horse artillery could see the Emperor of the French. Mists were rising from the plain that separated the

Anglo-Dutch position on the heights of Mont St. Jean and the inn called La Belle Alliance, a few hundred yards away, where Napoleon was standing. Mercer's gunners began to fire in that direction, and one shot fell not far from the little group of staff officers clustered around the emperor. When the French artillery opened up, the Anglo-Dutch guns all along the ridge began a general cannonade. The French stopped firing. Their mission was fulfilled - to see whether the whole enemy army had taken up position there. It had.

Both sides settled down for the night and the coming day's battle. It was a miserable night for everyone. The rain kept falling. The clayey ground was sodden. There was almost no food, although most of the men tried to warm themselves with tots of brandy or rum. Those Anglo-Dutch forces that were stationed in front of the great beech forest of Soignies managed to kindle fires of a kind, but the troops in the plain were less lucky. "We sat on our knapsacks until daylight without fires," recalled Sergeant Wheeler of the British infantry. "The water ran in streams from the cuffs of our jackets; in short, we were wet as if we had been plunged over head in a river. We had one consolation; we knew the enemy [was] in the same plight. The morning of the 18th June broke upon us and found us drenched with rain, benumbed and shaking with cold." Many of the

French infantrymen had lost their shoes in the sticky mud and were forced to bivouac in bare feet. On both sides, the muskets were so saturated that they were unusable. Neither army was in any condition to fight one of the most decisive battles in modern history. Yet fight it they did.

At 2:00 a.m., at the cramped, smoky little inn in the village of Waterloo, which he had made his headquarters, Wellington at last received word from Blücher. Field Marshal Gneisenau and Quartermaster General Karl von Grolman had held a lengthy discussion about the Prussian army's next move. By now, Gneisenau favored a retreat toward the Prussian line of communications, away from Wellington's army. But Blücher, supported by Grolman, opposed his chief of staff and made the final decision: The Prussians would support Wellington not with a single corps but with virtually their entire army. Only one corps would remain at Wavre to defend the town against a possible threat by Grouchy, moving north from Gembloux. The field marshal, who had recovered his stamina and his wits within an astonishingly-short time, had also achieved a triumph of good discipline. He had succeeded in rallying his army, soundly defeated only two days before but in good enough shape to mount another attack.

Sir Henry Hardinge, Wellington's liaison officer with the Prussians, recalled afterward that decisive night at Wavre. His left hand had been shattered by a bullet at Ligny, and he passed an uncomfortable night "with my amputated arm lying with some straw in Blücher's anteroom, Gneisenau and other generals constantly passing to and fro. Next morning, Blücher sent for me, calling me *Lieber Freund*, &c., and embracing me. I perceived he smelt most strongly of gin and of rhubarb. He said to me '*Ich stinke etwas*' ["I'm afraid I stink a little"] and that he had been obliged to take medicines, having been twice ridden over by the cavalry but that he should be quite satisfied if in conjunction with the Duke of Wellington he was able now to defeat his old enemy."

The message Blücher now sent Wellington was that Bülow's corps - which had arrived too late to take part in the Battle of Ligny - would march to the duke's assistance at daybreak on the eighteenth. It would be followed immediately by General George von Pirch's corps; the two other corps would follow later, as they had to rest from their fatigue. This was at least twice and perhaps four times as much help as Wellington had asked for. The duke, who had decided to fight only a rear guard action and to continue his retreat unless he received aid from the Prussians, now made up his mind to give battle in the morning.

Of this latest development, Napoleon had not the least inkling. He might have been informed of it if something had not gone wrong with Marshal Grouchy's pursuit of the Prussians. Even worse, something had gone wrong with his own communications with Marshal Grouchy. The crucial advantage of June 15 and 16 - the separation of the Prussian from the Anglo-Dutch forces - had been thrown away, and the emperor did not even know it.

6
"A HEAP OF GLORY"

It was with great reluctance that Marshal Grouchy had accepted the command of Napoleon's right wing. He was not experienced in handling troops other than cavalry, and he was a naturally cautious man who lacked the daring that made Napoleon such a remarkable commander. On the afternoon of June 17, Grouchy's corps was trapped in the same downpour that slowed the French advance beyond Quatre Bras, but he failed to keep his men moving. Not until 7:00 p.m. did his first troops reach Gembloux; it had taken them seven hours to march the six miles from Ligny.

At ten that evening, Grouchy sent a report to Napoleon that gave the emperor some strangely-inaccurate information. The Prussians, Grouchy reported, appeared to be retreating in three columns - one by way of Wavre to the north, one by way of Perwez to the northeast, and the third by way of Namur to Liège and the east. He assured his commander in chief that he would follow the main body of Blücher's troops the next day as soon as he had found out where it was headed. In his report, Grouchy mentioned the possibility that the Prussians might be planning to join up with Wellington. It did not occur to him, however, that if this were the case he would do much better to abandon his pursuit and return to add his 33,000 men to the emperor's forces. As for Napoleon, he was so far from realizing the Prussian potential for an attack he did not even bother to tell Grouchy that he himself was face to face with the Anglo-Dutch forces and expected to do battle the next day.

The emperor's only worry during that rainy night of June 17-18 was that Wellington might give him the slip. To make sure that this did not happen, he made the rounds of the French outposts in person. When dawn broke and he realized that the Anglo-Dutch army was still on the heights of Mont St. Jean, he felt he held victory in his hands. "Ah! Now I've got them, those English!" he exclaimed.

Early on June 18, the rain finally stopped, and Napoleon set the opening of the battle for six o'clock. After sunrise, however, his artillery expert suggested a postponement. The terrain was still too soggy for artillery or cavalry to maneuver successfully; a two- or three-hour-long wait would allow the ground to dry off under wind and sun. But even at nine, the ground was still sodden, and the opening of the battle had to be postponed again. From a low hill, the emperor, surrounded by a knot of generals, proudly surveyed his troops. The French were drawn up in position on a low ridge parallel to the somewhat higher crest of Mont St. Jean, and in full view of Wellington's army, barely 1,000 yards away. Napoleon's plan was simple: The main body of his troops would attack Wellington's position all along the line while Lobau's corps would push directly through the Anglo-Dutch center and cut off their retreat. The Imperial Guard, as usual, would remain in reserve. Arranged for a massive attack, the compact front of the 74,000-man French force was less than three miles long.

The emperor was confident of victory. "We have ninety chances in our favor," he remarked, "and not ten against us." Some of his generals, especially those who had fought Wellington in Spain, expressed their doubts. Marshal Soult suggested that Napoleon would be wise to call back Grouchy's 33,000 men in order to obtain a more-decisive superiority. The emperor derided him. "Just because you have been beaten by Wellington," he said, "you think he's a good general. But I tell you that Wellington is a bad general, and the English are bad troops." The entire affair, Napoleon boasted, would be a picnic for the French.

General Reille, another veteran of the Peninsular War, joined in. From his experience of Wellington's methods and of the quality of British troops, he felt sure that a frontal attack against them would be repulsed. He advised a simultaneous attack from the west to turn the Anglo-Dutch right flank. Napoleon, who disliked both timidity and criticism, ignored Reille's remark.

But now Prince Jérôme, Napoleon's youngest brother, came forward with some disquieting news. Jérôme had eaten dinner the night before at the same inn on the Charleroi-Brussels road where the Duke of Wellington and his staff had stopped for lunch. The waiter serving Jérôme had earlier heard one of the duke's aides mention that the British were planning to make a joint stand with the Prussians in front of the forest of Soignies. The Prussians, in fact, were already concentrating at Wavre for that purpose. Napoleon scoffed at this information as well. He simply refused to consider the possibility of a Prussian offensive move.

At 10:00 a.m., Napoleon finally dictated his instructions to Grouchy. He drew the marshal's attention to the fact that a large body of Prussian troops had been reported at Wavre. He ordered him to head for Wavre with all possible speed, to establish contact with the Prussians, and to push them before him. This order, too, was unclear. Presumably Napoleon wanted Grouchy to separate the Prussians from the Anglo-Dutch forces and drive them off to the east. In effect, however, he was ordering Grouchy not to prevent a Prussian junction with Wellington, but to drive Blücher directly into Wellington's arms. Grouchy can be blamed for not having used his head, but Napoleon cannot be excused from having given vague orders to a subordinate who he knew did not operate well on his own. Confidence had made the emperor careless.

The Duke of Wellington was as optimistic as Napoleon. He had positioned his 68,000 men in a masterly fashion. His troops and artillery were so well concealed that, for a while, the emperor believed Wellington might have retreated after all, leaving only a rear guard. Where Napoleon relied on a massive onslaught in heavy columns, Wellington counted on the staying power of his British and Hanoverian troops although he was unsure of the Dutch-Belgian ones. He disposed his hidden forces in a long, thin line whose effectiveness the French would discover only when their attack was launched.

Wellington, however, was overconfident in believing that a single Prussian corps would be sufficient to help him beat Napoleon. They had never faced each other on the battlefield, and each man underestimated the other. Blücher had been beaten by Napoleon often enough to respect the emperor almost as much as he hated him. Wisely, the field marshal took the risk of sending every man he could spare to the duke's assistance, leaving only General Johann von Thielmann's corps at Wavre to hold off Grouchy. Of his remaining three corps, Bülow's would join Wellington first while the two others fell on Napoleon's right flank. At about 9:30 a.m., Blücher dispatched a message to Baron von Muffling, Prussian liaison officer at Wellington's headquarters. "Ill as I am," the field marshal said, "I will march at the head of my army and will at once attack the enemy's right wing, should Napoleon attempt anything against the duke."

Although Blücher made the right decision, he and his staff made some slips in carrying it out. Bülow's corps had been chosen to serve as vanguard of the Prussian army because his troops were fresh. But his men were bivouacked to the east of Wavre, which meant they would have farther to march than the other three corps. They set off well before dawn but were delayed - first by a fire that broke out as they were marching through the streets of Wavre and then by the almost-impossible labor of forcing the heavy gun carriages and ammunition wagons along the narrow roads. Little better than rutted cart tracks at best, the twisting country lanes had been turned by the downpour into quagmires in which horses and men bogged down helplessly.

Knowing how critical Wellington's situation would be if Bülow reached him too late, Blücher rode in person to join the advance columns and spur them on their march. "Forward, my lads," he cried to them, "you won't let me break my word!" The lads tried their best, but they would never have joined the battle in time if Napoleon had not been obliged to delay his opening attack until 11:30 a.m. - five and a half hours later than planned. It seemed that even the weather was conspiring for the emperor's ruin.

The tall rye in the fields below Mont St. Jean could not conceal the French from their entrenched adversaries above. Indeed, in displaying his entire army before the Anglo-Dutch forces, Napoleon had hoped to demoralize his enemy. Wellington, of course, had no intention of opening the battle himself. He was still waiting for Bülow, and the later the battle began, the better it suited him. At 10:00 a.m., as Wellington watched through his spyglass, Napoleon rode past his troops drawn up for action and acknowledged their frenzied cheers of "*Vive l'Empereur!*" To the thunder of drum rolls and martial music from the bands, interspersed with trumpet calls, the infantrymen raised their shakos (caps) and their muskets, the cavalrymen their plumed helmets and sabers, to salute their great leader.

On the slopes of Mont St. Jean, nothing stirred.

At 11:30, the French began to move. From Wellington's vantage point, the sight was impressive, indeed. With the regularity and precision of a parade-ground drill, General Reille's corps advanced against the Allied right while skirmishers on their flanks covered them in the proper manner and gun batteries moved up to support the attack with their fire. The British guns responded promptly, accurately, and devastatingly. Within minutes, the battle was fully engaged.

The battlefield of Waterloo is crisscrossed by hedgerows, by the Charleroi-Brussels highway, and by various lesser roads. It is a gentle, rolling land of hillocks and hollows. Rye still grows to a remarkable height all over a countryside also dotted with orchards and prosperous farms. It is a peaceful landscape; yet here 45,000 men and 15,000 horses were killed and wounded - and most of them were buried - in an area of barely three square miles.

Within this narrow space on June 18, 1815, 140,000 men, and 30,000 horses sweated and struggled amid the roar of more than 400 guns. Smokeless powder had not yet been invented, and a thick pall of gunsmoke, made even thicker by the smoke of burning buildings, hung over the entire scene after the first two hours of battle.

Added to this discomfort was the sodden condition of the soil that under the tramp of soldiers' boots and horses' ironshod hoofs soon turned to mud. The thunder of the cannons, the incessant crackle of musket fire, the furious shouts of the charging soldiers, the screams for help from the mounds of dying and wounded, and the animal grunts of men locked in hand-to-hand combat - all these combined to produce an almost unbearable terror for those fighting. Yet the two opposing commanders could survey the scene from their respective command posts - only a mile or so apart - with the greatest coolness and composure.

Neither Wellington nor Napoleon was sentimental about spending human lives. But whereas Napoleon was used to handling armies of hundreds of thousands and to ruling almost a whole continent, Wellington's experience had been in leading much smaller forces against superior adversaries. As a result, he was more economical with his manpower and had developed tactics calculated to exploit every feature of the terrain and to make every soldier and gun count. With about 6,000 men fewer than Napoleon, the duke intended to stand his ground until the arrival of Prussian reinforcements. The position he had chosen was ideally suited for this purpose. The bulk of his forces was concealed behind the ridge of Mont St. Jean.

Expecting Napoleon's main attack to fall, as it did, on his center, he had selected two strong forward positions: on his right (west), the chateau and farm of Hougoumont, garrisoned by 1,200 British and Hanoverian troops; in the valley directly below his center, the small farm of La Haye Sainte, with a garrison of 400 men. Convinced that Napoleon would try to turn his vulnerable right flank, Wellington had weakened his total strength by diverting a reserve of 17,000 men to the village of Hal, nine miles west of the battleground. Even when it became obvious that the emperor had staked everything on an attack from the front, Wellington failed to recall the troops from Hal.

Napoleon mistakenly believed that Wellington's forces were superior to his. Yet Napoleon was convinced that, like almost every enemy he had faced, they would be too frightened to resist a massive frontal assault. He, therefore, chose to attack with columns massed in depth - a very costly way of fighting if the enemy did *not* turn and run. It was as if, on that day, he had made up his mind to risk all in one brutal blow and end the campaign with a thunderbolt.

The assault on Hougoumont, which opened the battle, had been intended by Napoleon as a mere diversion to draw away some of Wellington's forces from the center, his main target. But Jérôme Bonaparte, whose division led the attack, misunderstood his brother's intention. For once in his life the indolent Jérôme showed desperate energy - at what happened to be the wrong time.

It should have been clear to Jérôme, after a few minutes, that Hougoumont was too strongly defended to be taken by assault. His troops should have bypassed the château and gone on to join the main attack. Yet despite the orders of General Reille, his corps commander, Jérôme refused to abandon the assault. Calling on battalion after battalion, he gradually involved a substantial part of the army in a fight that should have been a mere feint. The struggle for Hougoumont raged all day. Hundreds of corpses piled up at the foot of its walls and in the surrounding woods. Eventually, on the emperor's orders, howitzers were brought up and began pouring their shells into the buildings, which caught fire. Shell explosions punctuated the screams of the wounded who had been dragged into the seeming safety of the farm buildings and were now trapped inside the blazing ruins. Retreating to the chapel and the main house, the defenders continued to hold out. Hougoumont remained in British hands throughout the battle.

Regardless of Jérôme's blunder, Napoleon had to proceed to the main phase of his thrust - the attack on the Allied center that had been planned for one o'clock. At noon, a massed battery of eighty-four French guns began a deafening cannonade to soften up the Allied position. Wellington's batteries immediately opened up in reply, but his infantry, which was placed rather close in front of its own guns, had to bear the brunt of the French fire. It was, an eyewitness reported, "a fire so terrible as to strike with awe the oldest veteran in the field." A Dutch-Belgian brigade had been drawn up by its commander, Major General Willem Frederik van Bylandt, in an exposed position on the slope facing the French. The cannonade took a terrible toll on Bylandt's men, who had to be withdrawn to a more protected area behind the ridge. There Wellington had carefully positioned the rest of his men so that the seasoned troops were interspersed with the less-experienced, and they stood their ground.

The cannonade had lasted an hour, and Ney, at one o'clock, was ready to lead d'Erlon's corps in a massed attack on Wellington's center. At that point, Napoleon noticed what seemed to be a black cloud issuing from the woods to the east of the battlefield, several miles away. It soon became obvious that the black cloud was a large body of troops - and the emperor, confident that these were Grouchy's men, dispatched a scouting patrol. It returned with the news that they were Prussians: The first units of Bülow's corps were arriving after a grueling march.

The emperor finally began to realize that his situation was critical. What had happened to Grouchy? How could he have let Bülow slip through his guard? Several years later, Napoleon wrote in his memoirs that it was "as if Grouchy's army had been surprised by an earthquake and swallowed up."

Whatever had happened to Grouchy, there was no time to lose. Napoleon was still unruffled. At 1:30, he ordered Ney to launch the attack on the Allied center, hoping that it would overwhelm the enemy before Bülow had time to intervene. "This morning," said the emperor to the officers surrounding him, "we had ninety chances out of a hundred in our favor. Bülow's arrival has cost us thirty, but we still have sixty against forty." Napoleon no longer had a choice. If he retreated, he was lost; if he attacked, he might conceivably still win. He attacked.

What *had* happened to Grouchy?

Like the emperor, he had slept little on the night of June 17-18. By 3:00 a.m., Grouchy had gathered enough intelligence to report to Napoleon from Gembloux that Blücher's main army seemed to be falling back toward Brussels to join with Wellington's forces. This message reached the emperor only about noon, and neither he nor Marshal Soult paid more than scant attention to it. They simply replied that Grouchy, keeping in close touch with Napoleon's headquarters, should try to prevent the Prussians from "annoying" the French right flank. The message had not yet been sent when, at 1:00 p.m., Bülow's corps appeared.

Soult at once added a postscript telling his fellow marshal that Bülow was approaching. "So do not lose a moment in drawing near to us and effecting a junction with us, in order to crush Bülow, whom you will catch in the very act of concentrating." This message was sent when Grouchy was at least fourteen miles from the battle while Bülow was already in sight. How could anyone but Napoleon, who always expected the impossible, suppose that Grouchy could receive the message in time to intercept Bülow?

But even in those days, there were faster ways for news to travel than by an orderly officer on horseback. At noon, Grouchy was having his lunch at Walhain, fourteen miles east of Waterloo, when he heard in the distance the formidable rumble of Napoleon's opening cannonade. With an effort, he might have covered the fourteen miles within four hours. Several of his staff officers urged him to march in the direction of the cannon fire whose intensity made it clear that a major battle was in progress. But Grouchy, unused to the heavy responsibility he was shouldering, insisted on sticking to his orders. As soon as lunch was over, he gave his men instructions to advance upon Wavre. By four o'clock, his forward units were hotly engaging the 16,000 Prussians left to guard the town. Although the emperor could not know it, there was no longer any possibility that Grouchy's corps could come to his aid.

As it happened, Bülow was not in a condition to launch an attack on the French right flank until after four. The other divisions of his corps did not straggle into the woods until mid-afternoon, and after their ordeal, the men needed time to rest and re-form. Napoleon, however, could not guess that the attack on his flank would be delayed for another three hours. He detached the 10,000 men of Lobau's corps, his reserve, to hold off Bülow, unnecessarily - and, as it turned out, fatally - weakening his striking force against the Allied center.

At 1:30, Ney finally launched his attack. With four divisions - 16,000 men in all - he and d'Erlon marched down the gentle slope from the inn of La Belle Alliance, across the plain, and began to mount the ridge opposite toward Mont St. Jean. As the men moved steadily through the chest-deep rye, their drums began the *pas de charge*, and the soldiers yelled *"Vive l'Empereur"* again and again. They advanced in huge columns, 200 men wide and at least twenty-four ranks deep - ideal targets for the Allied artillery that could mow down whole rows of men with grapeshot or well-directed nine-pound cannon balls.

From his command post on a hill a little behind La Belle Alliance, Napoleon watched the progress of his men. He alternately paced up and down, his thumbs in his waistcoat, or sat at a small table covered with maps. Beside him stood a local farmer named Decoster, who had been pressed into service as a guide. Napoleon questioned him constantly about the lie of the land, taking huge pinches of snuff all the while.

D'Erlon's men stormed up the ridge opposite, with Wellington's artillery slashing into them. Doggedly they continued their advance, closing ranks and leaving the fallen men behind. "No man has been better served by his soldiers," Napoleon said later. Perhaps no man should be that well-served. The defenders of La Haye Sainte beat off the attack with withering fire, but the central body of the French simply bypassed the farm and continued its ascent. Immediately ahead of them was Colonel Bylandt's Dutch-Belgian brigade that had lost one out of every four men in the earlier artillery cannonade. Bylandt's men fired one ragged, hysterical volley and fled in confusion to seek shelter to the rear.

Along the top of the ridge ran a narrow country lane, sunk between thick hedgerows that led from Hougoumont across the Charleroi-Brussels road in the direction of Wavre. As the central columns of Frenchmen, 8,000 strong, reached the ridge's crest, General Sir Thomas Picton's British infantry division suddenly rose from behind the hedgerows. Although depleted by the previous day's fighting at Quatre Bras, it was able to fill the gap so unexpectedly left by Bylandt's fleeing soldiers. With superb discipline, Picton's men had waited until the French were twenty yards away; then, with a cheer, they let loose a devastating musket volley. The French were too closely-packed to be able to return it effectively. As his enemy's front ranks crumbled, Picton ordered a bayonet charge and immediately fell dead from his horse with a bullet through his head. His battalions, however, charged down the slopes, pushing the French before them. To the left, the Highland Brigade, made up mainly of Scottish regiments, was outnumbered by almost eight to one and began falling back.

Wellington's heavy cavalry, the Union and Household brigades, went into action to turn the tide. Lord Uxbridge put himself at their head, and the trumpets blared. With thundering hoofs and wild cheers, the flower of the British cavalry charged forward into the struggling mass, shouting to the Allied infantry battalions to wheel aside and let them through. The Scots Greys, every rider mounted on a magnificent gray horse, yelled "Scotland forever!" as they charged down the slope. Some of their countrymen in the Highland Brigade grabbed hold of their stirrups and were carried forward in the mad rush, slashing to right and left at the demoralized Frenchmen. Somewhere amid the smoke sounded the skirl of bagpipes. Corporal Dickson of the Greys "plainly saw my old friend Pipe-Major Cameron standing apart on a hillock coolly playing 'Johnny Cope,

Are Ye Waukin' [waking] Yet' among all the din."
His colonel was in the lead, Dickson's account
continued, "past our guns and down the slope,
and we followed. . . . Just then I saw the first
Frenchman. A young officer of Fusiliers made a
slash at me with his sword, but I parried it and
broke his arm; the next second we were in the
thick of them. We could not see five yards ahead
for the smoke. . . . The French were fighting like
tigers . . . [but] as we were sweeping down a steep
slope on the top of them, they had to give way.
Then those in front began to cry out for 'quarter,'
throwing down their muskets. . . . The battalions
seemed to open out for us to pass through, and so
it happened that in five minutes we had cut our
way through as many thousands of Frenchmen."

In the impetus of the great charge, discipline
was lost. Excited almost beyond bearing by their
complete rout of the main French attack, the two
cavalry brigades charged on. "We dashed toward
the batteries on the ridge above, which had worked
such havoc on our ranks," Corporal Dickson wrote.
"The ground was very difficult and especially
where we crossed the edge of a ploughed field, so
that our horses sank to the knees as we struggled
on. . . . Then we got among the guns, and we had
our revenge. Such slaughtering! We sabered the
gunners [and] lamed the horses. . . . I can hear the
Frenchmen yet crying '*Diable!*' when I struck at
them, and the long-drawn hiss through their teeth

as my sword went home. Fifteen of their guns could not be fired again that day. The artillery drivers sat on their horses weeping aloud as we went among them; they were mere boys, we thought."

But in making havoc of Napoleon's great central battery, the cavalrymen had advanced too far. The French had taken a severe toll of both men and horses. Leaderless, their colonels dead and dying, the British cavalry brigades were trying to re-form when a vigorous French counterattack fell upon them and cut them to pieces. Their retreat covered by the few of their comrades who had remained in reserve, the remnants of Wellington's 2,000 heavy cavalry limped back to their positions. More than 800 of his best men and at least 1,000 horses were left behind.

When Uxbridge, as the duke's second in command, returned to his leader's vantage point under an elm tree, he found him surrounded by the attachés of the Allied powers, all resplendent in gold braid and in excellent spirits - unlike Uxbridge himself. Appalled by the disaster, he reproached himself bitterly for having lost control of the attack by leading it in person. Isolated from his reserves, with his commands to rally unheard in the din, he had totally lost control over his men. Yet the group around the duke, impressed only with the heavy casualties inflicted on the French, was convinced that the magnificent charge had turned the tide.

"I never saw so joyous a group," Uxbridge was to recall. "They thought the battle was over." But it was not over by any means.

Before the struggle began, Napoleon had told his staff how he would attack the Anglo-Dutch position. "I shall hammer them with my artillery, charge them with my cavalry to make them show themselves, and when I am quite sure where the actual English are, I shall go straight at them with my Guard." He now ordered Ney to renew the attack, this time with cavalry, on the Allied center. No one understood the value of artillery better than the emperor, who had begun his career as a gunner.

Accordingly, the fresh onslaught began with the biggest and most furious cannonade the world had thus far witnessed. The entire Anglo-Dutch infantry lay down flat on the ground to try to escape the hammering, but the fire was so accurate that they suffered fearful casualties all the same. Wellington, who had nearly a hundred fewer guns - and those of lighter caliber - than the French, ordered up his last artillery reserves to retaliate.

Captain Mercer, moving with his battery of horse artillery into a front-line position, felt as if he were entering an oven. The dense clouds of gunsmoke that enveloped the whole area made it hard to tell what was happening. "Despite the incessant roar of cannon and musketry," Mercer wrote, "[we] could distinctly hear around us a mysterious humming noise, like that . . . from myriads of black beetles; cannon shot, too, ploughed the ground in all directions, and so thick was the hail of balls and bullets that it seemed dangerous to extend the arm lest it be torn off."

The Brunswick troops, among whom Mercer's men had set up their guns, were absolutely terrified. These German boys, raw recruits, had taken severe punishment at Quatre Bras and had seen their revered leader, the Duke of Brunswick, shot down almost as soon as they entered the battle. Mercer observed that they "were falling fast - a shot every moment making great gaps in their squares, which the officers and sergeants were actively employed in filling up by pushing their men together, and sometimes thumping them ere they would move."

In an effort to give them fresh heart, Mercer deliberately disobeyed the duke's orders that the artillery seek refuge within the infantry squares as the enemy attacked. Instead, he and his men double-loaded their guns and stood in the open to await the French.

With the courage of a madman, Ney was meanwhile charging up the slope, straight at the Allied lines. Behind him came some 5,000 heavy cavalry armed with carbines and sabers. The Anglo-Dutch forces were arranged in oblong squares like a checkerboard to resist them, and the Allied batteries placed between the infantry battalions let fly with a storm of shrapnel and case shot. The front lines of Frenchmen broke, and horses fell, shattered and screaming, but still the cavalry came on.

The square, however, was the ideal defensive position for the British as long as the men comprising it kept their courage and allowed no gap to appear. The outer rank, on one knee, supported their musket butts on the ground so that their bayonets formed an almost-impenetrable barrier. The inner ranks, standing behind their comrades, could fire steadily over their heads. Within each square was a makeshift hospital, described by one guardsman as a "shocking sight. Inside we were nearly suffocated by the smoke and smell from burnt cartridges. It was impossible to move a yard without treading upon a wounded comrade, or upon the bodies of the dead."

The French cuirassiers swarmed in between and around the squares, firing off their carbines, trying to get the infantrymen to respond, but all to no purpose. They could not get close enough to do real damage, and the discipline of the square was strong enough to make the men in it hold their fire until a regular volley could be aimed at a mass of horsemen - with deadly effect. Finally, a counterattack by Uxbridge's cavalry threw the French back into the valley. "Never," wrote an English witness, "did cavalry behave so nobly, or was received by infantry so firmly." The result of all this nobility and firmness was several thousand more casualties, with nothing gained for either side.

It had been Ney's foolhardy choice to use unsupported cavalry for his charge. Misled by Wellington's apparent withdrawal of his men in the face of the French artillery pounding, he had believed the Anglo-Dutch forces to be retreating.

After a second futile attack, it became obvious they were doing no such thing, but Ney charged yet again, with an even vaster body of horses. Once more the French batteries softened up the enemy lines with a fearful cannonade. Men in the Allied squares, weary of standing their ground to be shot at, positively welcomed the arrival of the new French cavalry wave because it put a stop to the gunfire. Crowded into the thousand yards between Wellington's advanced posts of Hougoumont and La Haye Sainte, 9,000 French cavalry rode up to the attack. The horses, packed like cattle in a pen, had no space to maneuver, and their riders threw away their scabbards. On a suicide mission like this, there would be no putting back of swords.

"This time," said Captain Mercer, "it was child's play. They could not even approach us in decent order, and we fired most deliberately." The slope of Mont St. Jean was already covered with dead, wounded, and dying. More piled up at a terrifying rate, along with the carcasses of thousands of horses. Wounded and riderless animals dashed about the field, squealing with panic and adding to the confusion. Ney's third horse was killed under him. Mounted on a fourth, he managed to rally his men for yet another attack. It, too, failed, and Ney was glimpsed by one observer furiously beating an abandoned British gun with his sword. Having virtually wiped out the French cavalry in four unsuccessful charges, the marshal now tried an attack with both cavalry and infantry. But Wellington had reinforced his artillery, and the Frenchmen were again driven back with heavy losses. "Never did I see such a pounding match," the duke remarked afterward.

It is astonishing that Napoleon allowed Ney's madness to go on. In earlier battles, the emperor had been quick to change tactics when one approach failed; now, a strange lethargy seemed to have overcome him.

In any case, he had something else to worry about. Blücher, responding to messages from Wellington that begged for a speedy Prussian attack on the French right wing, insisted that Bülow advance what troops he had, unprepared though they were. At 4:30, the Prussians, expected by Wellington since midmorning, finally joined in the action. Lobau's corps, which Napoleon had sent to hold them off, was outnumbered three to one and fell slowly back.

The Prussians captured Plancenoit, a small hamlet on Napoleon's right flank. From there, their guns, hauled with such effort along the muddy lanes from Wavre, could fire along the Charleroi road, close to Napoleon's command post at La Belle Alliance. This added crossfire threatened not only to sever the French from their ammunition but to cut off their line of retreat.

Seeing this, the emperor ordered forward his Young Guard, the most junior members of his treasured reserve, to stem the tide. They retook the village of Plancenoit from the Prussians and drove them back to the shelter of the woods once more. But it was now after six o'clock, and a second Prussian corps - Pirch's - was already entering the woods from the east to support Bülow. Moreover, the advance guard of Zieten's corps was steadily nearing Wellington's positions farther to the north. The corps remaining at Wavre was having trouble holding off Grouchy and his men, and their commander, General Johann von Thielmann, sent a message to Gneisenau asking for help. Rather harshly, Gneisenau replied: "Let Thielmann defend himself as best he can; it matters little if he is crushed at Wavre so long as we gain the victory here." As if to echo those words, Bülow launched another attack upon Plancenoit and once more forced the French to abandon the village.

By 6:30, Napoleon's situation seemed desperate.

His initial great infantry attack on Wellington's center had been repulsed. Four massive cavalry charges had failed in turn. A joint infantry-cavalry attack had been scattered into wild disorder. The Prussians were threatening to turn his right flank, and his reserves were almost gone. Yet it was at this point that Napoleon very nearly won the battle.

The farm of La Haye Sainte was the key to Wellington's center. A bare hundred yards to the front of the main Allied position on Mont St. Jean, La Haye Sainte had been held bravely against incredible odds by one battalion of the King's German Legion under a British commander, Major Georg Baring. Again and again the defenders had been driven from the barn and outbuildings surrounding the little farm yet had rallied and retaken them from the French. Fires had started in the thatched roofs, but chains of men with soup kettles of water had managed to put them out. Baring had sent request after request to his commander in chief for more ammunition, but although Wellington had reinforced him with isolated companies of troops, no ammunition had been received. Toward evening, the little band of men with Baring discovered that they were down to three or four rounds of ammunition apiece. Holding a quick council of war, they decided to resist to the last man rather than withdraw from an outpost that could be infinitely valuable to the French.

Napoleon ordered Ney to bring up his men and take La Haye Sainte at all costs. This time, Ney was successful. The tiny garrison fought bravely to the very end, surrendering each doorway and corridor only after hand-to-hand fighting. But despite their heroic resistance, they were obliged to abandon the farm to Ney's infantry. Of the 400 defenders of La Haye Sainte, only forty-three, including Major Baring, made their way back to their own lines.

The engineers swarmed all over the farm, rapidly turning it into a fortified outpost for the French. Covered by skirmishers and supported by artillery moved to the farmyard, Ney's men at last were in a position to threaten Wellington's center. The Anglo-Dutch troops began to disintegrate under an attack from close range. The Prince of Orange, inexperienced and reckless, ordered first one regiment then another to break up its squares and deploy to drive off the French infantry. No sooner had each done so than Ney's cavalry came up and literally wiped out the unprotected troops. A whole regiment of Belgians turned tail and were only prevented from escaping by the Duke of Wellington himself, who came riding up with a squadron of dragoons to head off their flight.

All that day, in fact, Wellington had been in the thick of the fight, rallying his men wherever they wavered, taking refuge in one square after another as the cavalry charges swirled around them.

Apparently he bore a charmed life, for one staff officer after another fell at his side while he himself passed on untouched. At this final climactic stage of the battle, he had only a few inexperienced Brunswickers to throw into the chasm in his center. Since all his senior officers there had fallen, the duke himself took command.

One more supreme effort, and Napoleon could win the battle after all. Wellington had used up all his reserves while the emperor had the regiments of his Middle Guard and Old Guard - the cream of his soldiers - intact. If Wellington had to retreat, the Prussians would have to retreat, too. With skill, the French could keep the two allies separated. Ney realized this chance and sent his aide-de-camp to Napoleon to beg for additional infantry so that he could exploit his success. But the emperor, at this critical point on which his entire fate depended, appeared to have lost his judgment. "Troops!" he exclaimed, on hearing Ney's request. "Troops! Where do you expect me to find them? Do you expect me to make them?" Only half an hour later - half an hour too late - did he finally make up his mind to throw his Guard into the battle.

By that time, Wellington had closed the gap in his center. The credit for doing this belongs in truth to Baron von Müffling, who acted as liaison officer between Wellington and the Prussians. Anxiously awaiting the arrival of his countrymen on the field, Muffling suddenly noticed that Zieten's corps, which had been visible for some time on Wellington's left, was turning south to join forces with Bülow and Pirch, instead of coming to aid the Anglo-Dutch troops in their extreme peril.

On his own initiative, Muffling galloped over to Zieten to beg him to change his line of march. "If your corps does not go to the duke's rescue, the battle is lost," he insisted to the general who reluctantly gave in to him. With Zieten's troops now moving directly westward to reinforce his left flank, the duke was able to reorganize his line, drawing in the reserves no longer needed to protect that flank in order to strengthen his center. By the time Napoleon launched his final attack, the Allied line stood firm once more.

It was seven o'clock and nearing sunset. Napoleon, realizing that he must risk everything on one final blow, dispatched two battalions of the Old Guard to recapture Plancenoit and prevent the Prussians from surrounding him. Then he ordered his aides to rally every available man for the attack on the Anglo-Dutch positions. To fill them with fresh hope, he insisted the false news be spread that Grouchy and his men were approaching to reinforce them from the east. His next commands were to bring forward the remainder of the Imperial Guard for the last majestic advance. The emperor himself led the beginning of the charge, only moving aside to let Ney lead them forward when they were a bare 600 yards from the enemy.

As the drums rolled for the charge, Ney's fifth horse was shot from under him. His face blackened with powder, his uniform in tatters, he led the Guard on foot up the slope toward the Allied lines. At 200 yards' distance, the Anglo-Dutch guns opened fire. The grapeshot mowed down entire files of the Guard, who closed ranks and kept on going. Their discipline was magnificent, and their advance seemed irresistible.

Wellington, informed by a royalist deserter of the exact point for their attack, was waiting for them. With him was one of his own picked regiments, the First Foot Guards, lying in the trampled corn behind a hedge. As the Imperial Guard, in close columns, seventy men in each rank, neared the top of the ridge, Wellington called out, "Stand up, Guards!" Fifteen hundred redcoats, leaping to their feet, let loose a murderous series of volleys. The French Imperial Guard, able to fire only 200 muskets at once in return because of their tight column formation, came to a halt, and the British charged them with fixed bayonets. But in the gathering dusk and smoke and the din of gunfire, they misheard their colonel recalling them. Some tried to form squares, others retreated, and in the general confusion of their withdrawal, the French began to re-form and advance once more.

At this point, Sir John Colborne, a brilliant officer who commanded one of the very few experienced British regiments present in full strength, acted on his own initiative. Ordering his men forward by the northeast corner of still-blazing Hougoumont, he positioned them four-deep parallel to the advancing columns of the Imperial Guard. Colborne's men riddled the whole length of the French flank with fierce volleys of musketry. At the same time, the British First Foot Guards on the crest opened up, and Napoleon's Imperial Guard, caught between two overwhelming fires, began to fall back.

The rest of the French troops, drawn up to the rear of the Guard, had been eagerly watching their progress. Victory seemed at hand. Then suddenly they saw the backward movement, and in an instant, their confidence turned to panic. "The Guard is falling back!" was the fateful cry that gave the signal for a general rout. The hopes of Grouchy's arrival were over - the troops on the French right were now plainly seen to be Prussians. Within minutes, the whole of Napoleon's army, except the Guard, turned into a crazed mass of fugitives. Seeing them flee, Wellington, from the height of the Mont St. Jean ridge, held his cocked hat high in the air as a signal for a general charge. All day his men had stood and endured - endlessly. Now with cheers and hunting calls, British, Hanoverians,

Brunswickers, Dutch, and Belgians came rushing down the slope as if it were a steeplechase. The French rout turned into a stampede, with men running blindly to the rear, clogging the roads, and throwing away their weapons to shouts of "Save your lives!" Soldiers who had fought all day with such incredible courage at last knew nothing but animal fear and the desperate instinct of survival.

Napoleon attempted briefly to rally his troops, but it was futile. He was forced to take refuge within one of the squares formed by his Guard. The three reserve battalions held steadfast against the onslaught of an entire army. Slowly they retreated, sacrificing their lives to protect their emperor until he reached his waiting escort on the Charleroi road and set off, amid crowds of fugitives, on his flight south to the French border. When the British shouted to the Guard's commander, General Pierre Cambronne, to surrender, Cambronne screamed the obscenity that made his name famous: "*Merde!*" Historians sometimes translate this as "The Guard dies but never surrenders."

It was long past nine o'clock when Wellington and Blücher met to congratulate each other near the inn of La Belle Alliance. Since Wellington could not speak German and Blücher could not speak English, the victorious leaders held their brief conversation in French, the language of their defeated enemy.

The pursuit of the French was entrusted to the Prussians who had marched until their feet were sore but had suffered relatively slight casualties. The exhausted Anglo-Dutch troops were to bivouac on a blood-soaked battlefield piled with dead and dying, and crazed and wounded men and horses. It was, for one English survivor, "the last, the greatest, and the most uncomfortable heap of glory" he had ever had a hand in.

For Wellington, dismounting stiffly from his horse that night at the tiny Waterloo inn he had made his behind-the-lines headquarters, one more task remained. He must write his dispatch to London, informing the government of the great and terrible victory that would make this Belgian village world famous.

7
END OF AN ERA

A ll distinctions of nationality disappeared on the Waterloo battlefield during the night of June 18-19, 1815. Thousands of wounded lay about untended; many were to be left there for nearly a week. As they lay dying, some silently, some crying out - in English, in German, in French, in Flemish, in Dutch - the neighborhood peasants stalked about the field, robbing the dead of their weapons, their watches, their purses, and even their clothes.

The sun rose on a truly appalling sight. Major Harry Smith of the 95th Rifles, a veteran of bloody battles in the Peninsular War and in America, said that he had never seen anything to be compared with it. "At Waterloo the whole field from right to left was a mass of dead bodies. In one spot, to the right of La Haye Sainte, the French cuirassiers were literally piled on each other; many soldiers not wounded lying under their horses; others, fearfully wounded, occasionally with their horses struggling upon their wounded bodies. The sight was sickening. . . . All over the field you saw officers, and as many soldiers as were permitted to leave the ranks, leaning and weeping over some dead or dying brother or comrade."

Wives and sweethearts were there too, tending the wounded and crying over the dead. There were also sightseers who arrived from Brussels in carriages to view the battlefield. They saw a mass of bleeding and disemboweled bodies, fields where the rye had been trampled into a bloody quagmire, and trees shattered by cannon balls. Discarded knapsacks, belts, hats, cartridges, cannon wadding, broken wheels, and battered weapons, littered the area.

The previous evening, Napoleon, creator of all this havoc, had ridden as far as Genappe, on his way to Quatre Bras. There his luxurious traveling carriage was waiting for him, but he had no sooner taken his seat inside it when the alarm went up: "The Prussians are coming!" The emperor was forced to leap on his horse once more, and he and his escort galloped off just as the Prussians entered the town. The panic was general, and French soldiers crowded the streets, trampling one another in mortal fear.

There was good reason for terror - in the excitement of the chase, the Prussians sabered to right and left without bothering to check whether the enemy was armed, or even whether the men they killed were, indeed, enemies. Gneisenau, with barely 4,000 cavalry, pursued a disorderly rabble of nearly 40,000 along the Charleroi road until it became clear that the French were so demoralized that there was no longer a possibility of their rallying.

At Charleroi, on June 19, the Prussians captured an astonishing amount of booty - much of it from the emperor's special carriage. There were several bales of ready-printed proclamations, dated from the royal palace at Brussels on June 17, announcing his victory over "these barbarians . . . who fly with rage and despair in their hearts." Napoleon had also brought along with him an 800-volume library, complete services of gold and silver plate, and, most impressive of all, a uniform that had 1 million francs' worth of diamonds stitched into the lining.

From the sale of the Waterloo booty, prize money was distributed to the Allied forces. The Duke of Wellington received £61,000 (worth, at that time, about $300,000); the humble privates and drummers in his army, on the other hand, received £2 11s. 4d. apiece (about $12), and their shares would have been smaller still if so many of them had not been killed.

Of the 74,000 men Napoleon had had at Waterloo,

25,000 had been killed or wounded and 8,000 more taken prisoner. Practically all of his guns and most of his horses had been lost. Ironically, the only part of his army that emerged almost unscathed was the detachment commanded by Marshal Grouchy. Hearing from a breathless messenger of the complete rout of the main French army, Grouchy this time maneuvered with ability and speed. His army retreated into France in good order.

By June 21, Napoleon had arrived in Paris, exhausted but still planning fresh offensives. With Grouchy's men and the survivors from Waterloo, with carriage horses dragging the guns, with the 100,000 men of the National Guard, he had visions of withstanding the Allies and once more calling the French nation to arms.

But the decision was no longer his to make. The politicians who led the nation saw nothing to be gained from continuing the war or from keeping Napoleon as emperor. The Prussians were already deep inside France, devastating the countryside as they advanced, and the other Allied armies were approaching. What was the point of resistance? The men in power agreed that it would be better to placate the Allies, secure the best peace terms they could, and get rid of Napoleon forever.

This time, the emperor made no difficulties about abdicating. On June 22, he signed a declaration that "my political life is over, and I proclaim my son, Napoleon II, Emperor of the French." But his wishes were ignored. A provisional government was formed, which immediately opened negotiations with the Allies. The unhappy King of Rome, then in Austria with his mother, was to die before he was twenty-two, without ever gaining a crown.

Once he had signed away his throne, Napoleon seemed to have lost his powers of decision. For several days, he lingered at the chateau of Malmaison, on the outskirts of Paris, which had been Josephine's favorite home. By June 29, the Prussians were only a few miles away and threatening to shoot him on sight. Napoleon at last fled to the coast with a small staff that was prepared to accompany him into exile to the United States or wherever else he chose.

On July 3, he arrived at the Atlantic port of Rochefort and began investigating ways of taking ship to America. But British vessels were already blockading the port, and their commander refused to grant him safe passage. At last, Napoleon decided to board HMS *Bellerophon* and throw himself on the generosity of his British victors. Somewhat naively, he believed he could enjoy the simple life of a country squire in England, where he could "taste the only consolation permitted to a man who once governed the world, that of associating with enlightened minds."

But when the *Bellerophon* arrived at Plymouth, the

emperor found the British less enlightened than he had hoped. The Allies were not prepared to risk a repetition of the escape from Elba. For his second exile, Napoleon was banished to the tiny British colony of St. Helena.

The fallen emperor was to live out the remaining six years of his life on this South Atlantic island 1,200 miles from the west coast of Africa. There, surrounded by a small and ever-dwindling group of companions and servants, he spent his time feuding bitterly with the British governor and dictating his memoirs. But as he took less and less exercise, in protest against the governor's denial of his liberties, he grew extremely fat and increasingly lethargic. Boredom and illness were gradually killing him, and he began to waste away from cancer of the stomach. On May 5, 1821, he died, with his first wife's name on his lips. One of the doctors who attended him remarked that "in death the face was the most splendid I ever beheld; it seemed marked for conquest."

Napoleon's memory had not died, however, and his own writings, as well as those of his companions in captivity, soon began to be published. And, with the real Napoleon dead, the Napoleon of legend was born - a legend that was to grow to such proportions that within twenty years, his body would be brought back to Paris and given a hero's burial as he had wished, "on the banks of the Seine, amidst the French people whom I have so greatly loved."

On July 7, 1815, the Allied troops entered Paris. A day behind them came Louis XVIII, in their baggage train, as his enemies put it. His return was Wellington's doing, for the Allies were by no means agreed on restoring Louis to the throne a second time. Nor were they agreed on peace terms. The Prussians were particularly vindictive and wanted to punish France for supporting Napoleon by carving the country up among her neighbors. By bringing Louis back to Paris so speedily, Wellington forestalled that possibility and forced the Allies to accept the Bourbon king as a figurehead ready at hand.

Even so, the peace treaty of 1815 was far more severe on France than the peace terms of 1814 had been. Her borders were cut back to those that had existed in 1790 - all the Napoleonic conquests were gone. An indemnity of 700 million francs - about half what the Prussians had wanted to exact - was imposed on the country, and an army of occupation remained on French soil until the money was paid off in 1818. In addition, many of the art treasures acquired during the revolution and the Napoleonic wars were to be restored to their original owners. The value of these works of art probably exceeded even that of the indemnity, and the French people, who had come to think of them as their own, bitterly resented having to return them.

The officers who had fought with Napoleon paid for their enthusiasm with imprisonment, exile, or death. The chief casualty was Marshal Ney, whom Louis XVIII had no choice but to court-martial. Ney had openly played him false, and for such treason, there was only one punishment. Ney met his end in front of a firing squad before the year 1815 was over. His fellow marshal, Grouchy, was also court-martialed, but his sentence was a lighter one: exile. Grouchy spent six years in the United States before being allowed to return to France.

For both Blücher and Wellington, Waterloo was the last great battle. Blücher spent some time in Paris involving himself with Prussian plans to take revenge on the French and threatening to blow up one of Paris's finest bridges, the Pont d'Iéna, that commemorated the crushing Prussian defeat in 1806. However, he was successfully thwarted by the Duke of Wellington, who, as Allied commander in chief in France, posted a permanent British sentry on the bridge to detect any attempts at demolition. It was not long before the aged field marshal began to feel his years, and he returned to Prussia to live in retirement. He died in 1819, at the age of seventy-seven.

Wellington himself was to live to a greater age than Blücher and to serve his country for the rest of his life as a politician. He became prime minister in 1828, but his stubborn resistance to change at a time of overwhelming need for parliamentary reform brought his government tumbling down two years later. He never again headed a cabinet.

On June 18, 1832, he had to be rescued in the London streets from a howling mob who - on the seventeenth anniversary of Waterloo - had forgotten the hero-general in their fury at the reactionary politician. Yet in 1852, when Wellington died at the age of eighty-three, his nation's last gesture to the man who had saved it from Napoleon Bonaparte was a state funeral worthy of a reigning monarch.

Who won the battle of Waterloo? The British? The Prussians? Experts still argue the question. Without Blücher's cooperation, Wellington would have been routed, it is true. But then he would never have tried to give battle had he not been promised Blücher's assistance, which became effective only at a critically-late moment.

Through whose fault did Napoleon lose? Through his own? Through Ney's? Through Grouchy's? Because of circumstances beyond control, such as the heavy rains? Many mistakes were made on both sides of the struggle, and until the last two hours of the battle, the errors had tended to cancel one another out. Perhaps the result should be ascribed to accident, or to Providence.

About one thing there can be no quarrel: Wellington's army lost nearly 20,000 men in killed and wounded in the Waterloo campaign; Blücher's army, about 26,000; and Napoleon lost about 44,000 at Ligny, Quatre Bras, and Waterloo. Altogether, almost 90,000 men - and this does not include the pathetic thousands of dead and mutilated horses that were butchered in quantities a modern stockyard could not rival. The cost was staggering. Was the victory over one man's ambition worth such efforts, such suffering, such emotion?

It was said at the time, and has been said ever since, that the fate of Europe hinged on the outcome of Waterloo. In the long run, however, the fate of Europe or of the world depends more on those who work and who reason than on those who kill and maim. Perhaps the most significant result of the Battle of Waterloo was that it ended the career of one of the most remarkable men the world has ever known. However, it also marked the beginning of a new kind of collaboration between allies in the effort to establish firm foundations for a lasting and universal world peace.

On the day that the Treaty of Paris was signed - November 20, 1815 - Britain, Austria, Russia, and Prussia signed another document, known as the Quadruple Alliance. This was an engagement to protect the balance of power set up by the treaty and to consult one another if it was threatened.

It was, in effect, an early version of the League of Nations, formed after World War I, and the United Nations that grew out of World War II.

The statesmen of the period - Castlereagh and Metternich at their head - hoped that this alliance would maintain the order that had been so seriously threatened by Napoleon's conquests. The peace-keeping attempt was well-intentioned but destined to failure because it was too reactionary. The clock could not be turned back.

The French Revolution, Napoleon's meteoric rise to power, the banding together of rival nations to resist him - all had changed Europe permanently. The balance of power set up after Waterloo lasted nearly a century, despite a ferment of liberalism in almost every European country. The nineteenth century was destined to be a period of revolution, industrial or political. In a very real sense, Waterloo marked not the beginning, as was the hope of its victors, but the end of an era.

Made in the USA
Middletown, DE
10 September 2023